Meeting Mr. Right

by Lisa Raftery

and Barbara Precourt

Harrison House ™

Published by
Harrison House Publishing
Tulsa, OK

May Julia's story
strengthen you to
believe for your
dreams!

Lisa
Raftery

Psalm 31:24

S.O.S. Online is a fictional name of a web group used in this novel and has no real-life connection to anything found on the Internet.

All information on STDs was gleaned from the Centers for Disease Control and Prevention website at http://www.cdc.gov.

To read Charles Perrault's story of Cinderella, referenced in this work, visit http://www.pitt.edu/~dash/type0510a.html#perrault.

15 14 13 12   10 9 8 7 6 5 4 3 2 1

Meeting Mr. Right

ISBN: 978-160683-494-7

Copyright © 2012 by Lisa Raftery and Barbara Precourt

Cover Photography: Scott Miller, Miller Photography Tulsa, OK
Cover Model: Olivia Ophus and Caleb Ophus
Cover Design: Christian Ophus

Published by Harrison House Publishers, Inc.

Endorsements

Reading this book really helped me understand the importance of waiting for my own Mr. Right. It explains what to do in situations where you could compromise what you believe. The fact that Julia understood what it felt like to be alone after a break up, really helped me to relate. The tools that she used, I have now put into my own life. I've been journaling to God just as Julia did in the book. It's helped me become closer to God, realizing that God is my first love; He is able to help me to say no to compromise, guiding me along in life, loving me more than anyone can. I don't need a boy to make me happy!

Taressa B., age 15

Julia's story provides a delightful yet honest portrayal of a young lady's struggle to listen to and follow God's calling in a secular and persuasive world. This book may springboard discussions on important topics, which are often difficult for parents to introduce. The issues in this novel are ones your teen will want to talk about in the context of the characters' lives, providing a nonthreatening way to reinforce a Biblical worldview. I applaud the authors for their willingness to address topics which are crucial to adolescent development and yet often neglected. I highly endorse this book for both teens and singles.

Melissa Hurst, Psy.D.
Doctor of Clinical Psychology

This novel is a must read for all teenage girls. Most teens grapple with issues regarding dating and getting emotionally and physically involved with the opposite sex. Through the main character, teenagers can relate to struggles that are very similar to their own, yet learn from Julia's mistakes. They also gain insights for making a right choice when their feelings are going in the wrong direction! I loved how Julia daily journaled to God, expressing all her frustrations and questions. It caused my teenager to desire a journal to do the same! It's been exciting to hear my daughter talk about what Julia did or didn't do. It has encouraged my teenager to wait for Mr. Right. Thank you for writing such an amazing book!

Pastor Tracy Boyd
Life Christian Church

This book is a great read! Not only is it filled with important pieces of advice for girls, but it also takes you on a spiritual journey alongside the main character, Julia. I believe that through reading this book, girls will learn important principles in decision-making, as well as how to guard their hearts while waiting for their own Mr. Right. I highly recommend this engaging novel!

Lindsay Russo
Founder of Angel House, Co-leader of Missions.Me

Dedication

Meeting Mr. Right is lovingly dedicated to the memory of Dorothy Margaret, Barbara's mother and Lisa's grandmother. She was one of the sweetest and most unselfish women we have ever known. Through the years, she modeled for us how to love and respect a husband in good as well as difficult times. This remarkable lady used a modest steel worker's income to transform a simple house into an inviting home, filling it with meaningful traditions and delicious meals. We always felt her love and approval, and she will forever hold a cherished place in our hearts.

Acknowledgements

We want to extend our deepest gratitude to the following people who helped make this novel possible:

Stephanie Precourt, for her assistance with the computer-sensitive areas of the book, as well as her helpful suggestions and enthusiasm.

Kim Sgouroudis and Lois Precourt, for their support and valuable input.

Pastors Larry and Victoria Raftery, for their prayers and constant support throughout this project.

Our husbands, Eric Raftery and Roger Precourt, for their continual encouragement and support.

Most of all, to our Heavenly Father, for giving us the privilege of writing this novel for Him.

Contents

Starting Over

What had started out as a drizzle was now a steady rainfall. Taking one hand off the steering wheel, I switched on the windshield wipers to better see the road ahead. The fragrance of the morning shower filtered in through a partially-opened window on the passenger side of the car.

Suddenly, I was swept back in time to the night Jay and I had walked back from the library in the rain. I could almost feel the wet clothes clinging to my body. Jay's goodnight kiss was still etched in my mind, the one that made us burst out laughing when his lips slipped off mine and onto my cheek. As happy as we were then, it was hard to believe how tragically things had ended between us.

But thankfully, that was all behind me now. It had been weeks since I had seen Jay; my father had forbidden him to contact me again. Even if I'd been

allowed to see him one last time, what would I have said? What was there to say? What he had done to me was inconceivable, and yet, not surprising.

These unexpected flashbacks with Jay were consequences of the wrong choices I had made my first year at college—choices that almost ended my life. Although I knew God had totally forgiven me, I was still dealing with painful memories.

It was almost a year ago that I packed up my car and drove to Tyler University to begin my first semester at college. My parents weren't happy about sending me to a school almost eight hours from home, but I had set my heart on that school, and they finally agreed to let me go.

Heading off to Tyler that day, my intentions were good. I hadn't planned on joining a sorority, compromising a lot of my Christian values, or purposely deceiving my parents and friends. But that's what I ended up doing my second semester.

Looking back, my problem started in high school when I began to envy others girls. They went to parties and dances with their boyfriends, but my parents wouldn't let me go. When I listened to the girls talk about how much fun they were having, I was secretly jealous. Some of them bragged about drinking and having sex, but I didn't want to do that. I just wanted a boyfriend and the freedom to make my own decisions.

I finally got my wish when I went away to school. What I didn't understand then was that too much freedom before you're ready can lead to making wrong choices. And the price tag for those choices is rarely marked ahead of time; the bill arrives *after* the damage has already been done.

The bill for my season of compromise had arrived, and I was now paying for it. My mistakes that first year made my dad realize I was still an immature girl who needed his supervision, and the offer to attend college away from home had been withdrawn. This morning I was on my way to the college in my home-town—the college I had promised myself I would *never* attend.

By the time I pulled onto the campus of Weston University, the rain had returned to a light mist. Today I would finalize my fall schedule and find out exactly which of my credits had transferred from Tyler. I was hoping that changing my major from English to Physical Therapy wouldn't put me even further behind. Physical therapists needed to complete graduate work in addition to a bachelor's degree, so that would mean I had at least five more years of school, maybe more, depending on how much of my first year transferred.

I drove around for a few minutes, trying to locate the Administration Building. Spotting it to my left, I turned into the nearest parking area and weaved down aisle after aisle until I finally found a space in the crowded lot.

Pulling my keys from the ignition, I quickly checked my hair and lipstick in the rearview mirror. With a hasty glance at my watch, I saw I'd have to hurry to avoid being late. Tossing my purse over my

shoulder, I jumped out of the car and bolted toward the old building.

Once inside, I easily found my way to the student advisors' waiting room. I barely had time to sit down before Mrs. Roberts entered and politely invited me into a small office. There we discussed my new major and classes for the fall semester. Unfortunately, only half of my credits from the year before had transferred, and that meant I was technically still a freshman.

Seeing how disappointed I was, my counselor tried to console me. "Cheer up, Julia. I know your classes didn't all transfer, but at least you're not changing your major two years from now. That would've *really* delayed your graduation."

Forcing a smile, I thanked the woman for all her help. After handing me a schedule, she directed me to the bursar's office to pay my tuition, and we shook hands goodbye.

When I reached the office on the third floor, there was already a group of students waiting. "Welcome back to college," I muttered under my breath as I took my place at the end of the line.

"You said it," someone agreed, stepping in line behind me.

I turned around and shyly put my hand up to my mouth. "Oh, sorry. I have a problem thinking out loud sometimes."

"Lucky you. I have a problem just thinkin'," the stranger confessed with a wink. "I go to school because my dad never had a chance to go. He wants me to do better than him, ya know? I'm majorin' in communications. I figure that after four years of studying this stuff, I'll be able to explain to my dad why I got this degree and yet still like workin' as a mechanic. That's all I really wanna do—work on cars. Hey, at least I'll be the best-speakin' guy at the garage. So, am I talkin' too much or what?"

I couldn't help but grin. He definitely *was* talking too much, but he seemed harmless enough. He actually bounced a little when he talked. Just as I was about to answer him, he kept going. "So, what's your name? They call me Flip."

"I'm Julia," I fired back before he could cut me off again.

"Julia, huh?" he said, scratching his head. "I think I had an aunt with that name once. But she was real old, and I never knew her much. You're the first Julia my age I ever knew. Makes ya think, don't it?"

This guy was a real character. Although I wasn't quite sure how this conversation got started, I felt I had to be polite. "So, why do they call you Flip?"

"Well, that's not my real name. My real name's Alvin Avery. My dad nicknamed me Flip 'cause he said I flip between thoughts all the time."

"Really?" I answered, trying to hide a smile.

"Yeah! I don't get it neither. It kinda worked out okay 'cause I like Flip a lot better than Alvin. Who wouldn't, ya know?" he said poking me, amused by his own humor.

Our conversation was suddenly interrupted with a loud, "Next, please." I looked over to see the woman working there motioning for me to step up to the counter. For the next few minutes, I was busy answering questions and writing out my check. When I finally turned to leave, Flip waved and said, "See ya 'round, Julia. Good talkin' to ya."

Walking out the door, I heard Flip greet the worker next, telling her all about the last time he'd been there to pay his tuition. I couldn't help but feel sorry for the student behind him in line. She was in for a long wait.

When I got outside the building, the rain clouds had already disappeared. Rolling my windows all the way down, I enjoyed the drive home in the bright sunshine. When I pulled into our driveway some fifteen minutes later, my dad was trimming a bush on the side of the house. Looking up, he wiped his brow with a handkerchief and called out, "How'd it go, sweetheart?"

I didn't answer. I just got out of the car, walked over, and gave him a hug. He planted a big kiss on my forehead and asked, "What's with the long face? Anything go wrong on campus today?"

"No, everything's fine. I'm all set to start classes there this fall."

"Then why so glum?"

"I'm not sure I can explain it, Dad. I'm just feeling a little bummed. It's like I wasted a whole year of my life, and I can't get it back. I almost feel like I'm starting over."

"Well, you are making a new start, Julia. How many of your classes transferred?"

"Only half of them."

"I'm sorry, honey. But what you lost doesn't compare with what you gained. You came away from your mistakes at college with a deeper desire for God and more wisdom on how to handle relationships. Don't look at what happened to you as a waste; build on it instead."

"I'll try," I promised.

"Besides, there's nothing wrong with you that one of your mother's lunches won't cure," my dad added confidently. "I think we're having burgers on the grill out back. I don't know about you, but I've worked up quite an appetite."

My dad put his arm around my shoulders and leisurely strolled with me down the curved, brick walkway that led to the rear patio, just off the kitchen. Lunch was already set out on the outdoor table. My mom was about to call out that the food was ready when she saw us rounding the corner. "Good timing you two. The burgers are done."

"I'll be with you ladies in a minute," my dad replied, walking toward the house. "I need to wash my hands first."

While he was cleaning up, I gave my mom an update on what had happened that morning. We were still laughing when my dad returned.

"Care to let me in on the joke?"

"Sure, right after you say the blessing. I'm starved!"

"Heavenly Father, bless this food and strengthen us for Your service. We thank you in Jesus' name. Okay,

now what was so funny?" he asked before taking a bite out of his hamburger.

I relayed the conversation I had waiting in line with Flip. Now my dad was laughing. "I'm sure he's the guy who worked on my car last week at the garage downtown. It must be him. He fits your description, and one of the other mechanics called him Flip."

When we were finished eating, I helped my mom carry the dishes inside and fill the dishwasher. My dad was right. Life looked a lot brighter on a full stomach.

My plan for the afternoon was to go through some boxes that were still stacked in the corner of my bedroom. My dad had packed up my things at the sorority house and brought them home ahead of me, so I had no idea what was in each box until I opened it. After sorting through these last four, my room would be back to normal. Anxious to get started, I grabbed a can of soda and ran upstairs.

Before beginning, I walked over to the window in my room and opened it, inviting in a gentle breeze. Then I popped in a CD and tackled the first box. As I meticulously worked away, I noticed that things had definitely fit better into my room *before* I went away to school. The bookcase above my desk seemed smaller now, and my drawers and walk-in closet were beginning to get that *can't-hold-much-more* look.

For the next hour or so, I reorganized my things and reminisced through pictures and letters from school. As I was flipping through one of my text-books, I noticed a sealed, white envelope sticking out from the pages. My mind started racing. *Where did this envelope come from? What could be inside?*

Without any further speculation, I ripped it open and found a folded piece of paper with three photographs. As I flipped through the pictures, each one revived events and feelings I was desperately trying to forget. Since I'd been home, seeing Jay's face had been limited to momentary flashbacks. Now I was looking at full-color images of him—both of us—together.

These were the pictures J.R. had taken with Jay's camera the night of the spring formal. Had Jason Wells actually been this handsome? Did I really look this lovely in that borrowed silk gown? To see the two of us here, one would think we were the ideal couple, very much in love. But for the whole truth, another picture was needed from our date one week later. Chills began running up and down my spine as I recalled that terrible night.

Shaking my head, I refused to think about it anymore. Even so, curiosity compelled me to unfold the note and read it:

> *Look at these pictures, Julia. Don't you see how in love we are? You can't run away from what's happened to us this last semester any more than I can. The next time we're in a picture together, it will be at our wedding. It's time to let go and say yes to what your heart wants.*

It didn't take me long to figure out where this envelope was inserted into my English book. It must have happened at the library, the day after the dance.

Jay had probably slipped it in there after I told him it was over between us. He apparently thought that seeing these pictures would convince me to marry him. Little did he know, I wouldn't even find them until the relationship was permanently severed and I was back home to stay.

Re-reading the note, I found myself reliving it all—the way Jay never seemed to hear any of my objections, his inability to take *no* for an answer, the charm tactics he used to get me to do what he wanted, the fact that no matter how I tried to guard myself against him, he could make me believe his lies...

Suddenly, my mom's voice calling from downstairs brought me back to the present. "The phone's for you, Julia!" I had been so deep in thought, I hadn't even heard it ring.

"I've got it, Mom," I shouted back as I picked up the receiver.

"What are you doing?" a voice asked.

"Still unpacking some boxes. Why?"

"I've got to run to the mall for a few things. Wanna go?"

"Sure. You driving?"

"Yeah, I'll pick you up in about ten minutes."

"Great. See you then."

I was grateful Cassie had called when she did. I needed to get away from the house and get Jay off my mind. Replacing the photos and note into the envelope, I stuffed it into my nightstand drawer. Then I changed my clothes, refreshed my makeup, and went downstairs.

When I reached the foyer, I saw my mom curled up in a chair in the living room, reading. She looked up from her book. "What did Cassie want?"

"We're going to the mall for a while."

"Dad and I have plans with the Emersons later, so you might want to grab something to eat while you're out."

"Okay, I'll have dinner with Cassie. Here she is now," I reported, looking out the sidelight by the front door. "Have fun tonight," I called over my shoulder as I ran out of the house.

Cassie was just pulling into the driveway. We lived a few blocks away from each other and had been best friends since elementary school. She had been so disappointed the year before when I decided to attend a college out of state. The oldest of five children, her parents couldn't afford to send her away to school. She had always envisioned both of us graduating from Weston University; now her dream was becoming a reality.

As I approached the car, Cassie rolled down the passenger window and greeted me. "What's the mission today?" I asked as I got inside and buckled my seat belt.

"To find some black heels at Dempsey's. I know that store's expensive, but I like their shoes." Noticing I looked a little down, she asked, "What's wrong?"

"My past keeps finding a way to resurface and torment me."

"Having a little Jay withdrawal, are we?"

"No, just a lot of regrets about him. I really don't want to get into it."

Cassie quickly changed the subject, and soon I found myself having fun and no longer thinking about Jay. After shopping for almost two hours, we remembered why we had come to the mall in the first place—black heels at Dempsey's! Cassie found exactly what she was looking for there, but they only had the shoes in brown. She settled for another pair on the sale rack that she liked almost as well.

On the way home, we grabbed some dinner at one of our favorite restaurants. As we sat in a booth talking and laughing, I silently thanked God for giving me such a great friend. She was like the sister I never had. Cassie, however, had no shortage in that department. She had *three* sisters and often felt sorry for her little brother being brought up in a house full of girls.

It was almost nine o'clock when I finally got back home. My parents were still out, and the house was quiet and peaceful. Tired from the day, I decided to turn in early and went directly upstairs.

I always felt like a princess in my room. I especially loved to stand out on my balcony and admire the beautiful woods behind our house. A large fountain ran constantly in the garden below, and on warm evenings, I would open my French doors and fall asleep to the sound of cascading waters.

This was such a night. After I'd finished unpacking the last box, I got ready for bed, opened the doors, and slipped between the sheets. As I listened to the fountain and the familiar sounds of the nighttime creatures still awake in the garden, I tried to enjoy the moment and not think about the next day.

In the morning, my brother, John, was coming for a visit with his wife. I hadn't seen the two of them since Christmas break last winter, so this would be the first time facing John since my big mess up at college. Our dad had only briefly explained to him what had happened; I wanted to tell him the whole story myself.

Even though John was six years older than me, the two of us had always been close, and I was anxious to finally talk to him about what had happened. He had a way of making things better, helping me to see the bright side. Even so, I was dreading my confession, still fighting feelings of shame and failure about Jay.

I remembered once telling a sorority sister that with God, she could live free from the past and start anew. Now I was finding it hard to follow my own advice.

Before falling asleep, I uttered a simple but sincere prayer: "*Lord, please help me to be more understanding when people are having a hard time emotionally. I know now these battles are not won without a struggle. It takes time to heal.*"

Bittersweet Reunion

It was already past eleven, and John and Jenny hadn't arrived yet. I had just taken a shower, and as I stepped out of the bathroom in my robe, I could see my mom across the hall in my brother's old room, busily changing the bed sheets.

"When did they say they'd be here?" she called out as she smoothed down the comforter.

My dad was just coming down the hall and answered her once he reached the doorway. "When John called last night, he said they'd be here by noon. That's the third time you've asked me that, my dear. If I didn't know any better, I'd say you couldn't wait to see them."

"Tease me if you want," my mom laughed, "but they haven't been home for ages, and I miss them."

"Me, too," I said as I turned and walked to my room to finish getting ready. Once inside, I closed the door behind me and sat down on my bed. Tentatively opening the drawer to my nightstand, I pulled out the white envelope that Jay had slipped into my book and carefully removed the three pictures that were inside. As I studied them, I felt a twinge in my spirit, much like the sick feeling I'd experienced when I agreed to go out on that last date with Jay.

What's the problem, Julia? I chided myself. *These are only pictures; Jay can't hurt you anymore. It's safe to remember one of the most romantic nights of your life. Just don't think about when he...*

My thoughts were interrupted by a noise in the hallway outside my room. Quickly, I jammed the pictures and note back into my nightstand, my heart beating wildly at the idea of being found with anything that would remind my dad of Jay.

When all was quiet and no one had rapped on my door, I realized that one of my parents must have brushed up against something on the way downstairs. The fear of discovery past, I let out a sigh of relief.

I rationalized that it wasn't wrong to hide these things in my room; after all, I was going to throw them away eventually, maybe after I had a chance to show them to Cassie. It would only upset my parents to see these things, so why cause them pain? In time, I could get rid of everything without my mom and dad knowing. But for now, my little secret was safely tucked away in my nightstand, and I could finish getting dressed.

About an hour later, I heard my dad call out that John and Jenny's car had pulled into the driveway.

Rushing downstairs, I joined my parents just as they were opening the front door.

John hugged my parents first and then turned to put his arm around me. "Hey, how's my favorite sister doing?" he asked, giving me a big kiss on the cheek.

"Better now that you're home," I replied, tearing up.

John hugged me close, knowing I was still hurting from whatever happened at Tyler. He could tell that while I was glad to see him, I wasn't happy about what I needed to explain. It was definitely a bitter-sweet reunion.

We spent the rest of the day as a family catching up and enjoying time together again. Then we went out for dinner and a few rounds of miniature golf. My dad won, as usual. How could the rest of us compete, with him playing golf almost every weekend with his clients?

The next morning we were all up and on the road by ten o'clock, headed to my grandparents' cottage for the week. Staring out the car window, I smiled at the thought of returning to their place. It was beautiful this time of year, and I always felt God's presence in a special way there. Somehow problems seemed to melt away by the mountains and peaceful river, and I hoped that my talk with John would bring me the encouragement I needed.

After a ninety-minute drive, we pulled our two cars up to the front steps of the cottage and jumped out to greet my mom's parents, who were sitting on the porch, waiting for us to arrive.

Grandma Helen had already prepared lunch, so after unloading the cars and putting our bags in our rooms, we all joined her and Grandpa Carl on the veranda out back. As I sat in the middle of the long wooden table watching my family laughing and having a wonderful time, I wished I could feel that happy, too.

When the meal was over, everyone pitched in to clear off the table and carry everything inside. Then the men left to go fishing while we women finished cleaning up the kitchen.

John's wife and I were assigned dish duty, and the whole time we worked together, I could feel her watching me. I even saw her start to say something a few times and then decide against it. Jenny and I had gotten pretty close the summer she lived with our family, and I knew she was trying to reach out to me without prying into my private life. She could tell I was hurting, but she didn't know any more than John did.

It wasn't until we were alone that afternoon, laying out on the river dock, that Jenny tried to get me to open up and say what was bothering me. Trying to be subtle, she simply asked, "Are you okay? You seem a little down."

"I knew I wasn't fooling you," I sighed, turning over onto my back. "I guess I'm not such a great actress after all."

"Do you want to talk about it?"

"Yes, but I want to wait for John so I don't have to say it all twice."

Trying to be sensitive, Jenny asked, "Would you rather talk to your brother alone?"

"Not really. He'd tell you about it later anyway. Besides, I respect your opinion. I want you to be there."

Jenny thought for a moment. "Tonight's not really a good time, is it?"

"No," I answered, remembering the game night already planned for after dinner. "What about tomorrow? The weather's supposed to be nice; we can take a picnic lunch to the cove and talk there. I'm sure Grandpa will let us use the pontoon."

While Jenny was nodding *okay*, we heard a shrill whistle coming from somewhere off shore. We smiled at each other, knowing it had to be John. Sure enough, the pontoon boat was just coming into view around a bend a few hundred feet away. When it reached the dock, we greeted the men, praising them for all the fish they'd caught. Then we gathered up our things and headed for the cottage to help with supper.

Two hours later, the family was seated at the table again, enjoying dinner. Once dessert and coffee had been served, John asked if he could have everyone's attention; he and Jenny had an announcement to make.

Surprised, we all turned towards him expectantly. Assuming he was going to say Jenny was pregnant, I sat stunned as my brother announced they were leaving in a few weeks for Chile, South America. John would be overseeing a big engineering project there, and Jenny would be working as a nurse in a local clinic. John explained how they had wanted to live in another country before having kids, and this was their chance.

I wanted to be happy for them, but now I felt lonelier than ever. How could they commit to be away from us for three years? Fighting back tears, I left the room as everyone else gathered around John and Jenny to congratulate them. That night while the rest of the family played games out on the porch, I went to bed early. I just couldn't fake being excited and happy when I wasn't.

It was almost noon the next day when John, Jenny, and I finally arrived at the cove just a few miles downstream from the cottage. With a beautiful waterfall and a picnic area our grandfather had added, this was the best spot to swim on the river and John's favorite place to relax.

After securing the pontoon to the dock, we all hopped off and carried the food and beach bags up to the deck. John immediately opened the shed, grabbed the charcoal bag, and got the grill started. As soon as the coals were hot, Jenny put some bratwurst on to cook while I set the remaining food out on the picnic table.

When we had finished eating and I still hadn't opened up, John decided it was time to stop the stalling. "Okay, sis. Are you ready to tell us what happened at school?"

"I guess that's why we're here," I answered sheepishly. "But first, what did Dad tell you?"

"Not much. Just that you'd had a bad dating experience your last semester and he felt you needed to come home and finish your degree at Weston U."

"I wish that was all there was to it," I lamented, embarrassed to have to admit the truth. For the next hour, I shared with Jenny and John why I got involved in sorority life, how I met Jay, and all about our dating relationship, including what he had done to me. I explained how Mom and Dad found out and why they had decided to bring me home. When I was finished, John came over and put his arm around me. "Wow! You have had a rough time of it, haven't you?"

By now I was crying, and Jenny hugged me next, trying to comfort me. But before Jenny could say anything, John took my hand and gave it a squeeze. "Will you forgive me, Julia?"

I looked up at him, startled. "Forgive you? For what? You didn't do anything."

"Sure I did. I knew you were going away to college with your head full of a bunch of romantic nonsense, and I never bothered to tell you what college life was like or how to avoid the wrong kind of guys. Believe me; after finishing grad school, I'd seen it all.

"That summer before you left home, I'd fallen in love with Jenny, and she was all I thought about. I was going half-crazy myself trying to work a twelve-hour day, help plan a wedding, and keep my passions for Jen under control. At first I was glad Mom and Dad let Jenny stay with us that summer before we got married. I didn't want her to have to live alone with her dad traveling all the time. But I've got to tell you, those were some of the most miserable months of my life."

I had stopped crying by this time, and my jaw dropped in amazement. "You've got to be joking!"

"No, I'm not. Do you want to know why? You may think of me as just your brother, Julia, but I'm a man. And men think about sex. *A lot.* More times a day than I'd like to admit, actually. That's the truth, and it's important you understand it. God created us this way; it's totally normal.

"Since we have such a strong sex drive, the devil does everything he can to accelerate and pervert it outside of marriage. I mean, a man is still a man, Julia—even though he's a Christian. The good news is God can help men control their thoughts and passions and show women the respect they deserve. Sad to say, some guys aren't willing to yield to Him in this area."

I still looked a bit shocked, but since I was listening attentively, John continued without waiting for a response. "Did you ever wonder why I lost so much weight the summer before Jen and I got married?"

I finally found my tongue. "I just figured you were working too hard."

"Well, mostly it was from running so many miles at night. After dinner, Jen and I would usually go and sit in the swing in the garden to have some privacy. As you might guess, some kissing went on out there, which got me all stirred up. Before long, we'd have to turn in for the night so I could be back on the jobsite early in the morning.

"So, I'd walk Jen to her bedroom and give her one last kiss. Then she'd close the door behind her, and the torment began. My room was exactly fifteen steps away from where Jenny was undressing. Trust me; I counted them every night. All the way down the hall, I tried not to think about what was happening in her room—what she was taking off, what she was putting on, how beautiful she must look lying in bed…

"But the worst part would come when I finally got into bed and my body would begin to ache for her. All I could think about was how great it would be to feel Jenny next to me and hold her close. When I shut my eyes, I could still smell her perfume and taste that last kiss.

"I couldn't lie there and think about her anymore; it was too frustrating. That's when I'd turn my light back on and read the Bible to get my mind off her. But many nights it didn't work, so I'd throw on some sweats and go running. Then I'd come back exhausted and fall into bed, too tired to get into any trouble." John paused for a moment and grinned at Jenny. "I'm glad we got married when we did. I don't think I could've survived much longer."

Jenny smiled back at John and jokingly punched his arm. Turning to me, she said, "I had no idea what your brother was going through. He didn't tell me about it until we were on our honeymoon. Because he didn't say anything, I had a hard time myself right before our wedding. I started to notice John wasn't as affectionate as usual, and it scared me. He was pulling back to help him cope, but since I didn't know that, I thought he was having second thoughts about getting married.

"I was so worried, I decided to confront him at dinner one night when we were alone. When I finally asked if we were still okay, he just looked at me and nodded. I was glad no one else was home because I broke down and started sobbing. It totally shocked your brother; he'd never seen me like that before. He kept asking me over and over what was wrong, what he'd done to upset me."

"I didn't know what to do!" John admitted. "She was crying so hard she couldn't talk. Finally, she said she was afraid I didn't love her. I remember thinking that if I loved her any more, I'd go crazy! But that wasn't what she needed to hear, so I just held her close and assured her I still loved her and always would. I didn't explain why I'd been so distant, figuring that in a week the struggle would be over and I could finally show my love for her sexually. All I had to do was make it through seven more days. I ran again that night and every night until our wedding.

"When it was all over, I was grateful that God had helped me get to the altar without compromising Jen's purity or my integrity. I was tired and a little thin, but I had honored my commitment to the Lord and proven myself worthy of Jen's love and trust."

"When John told me all this," Jenny added, "I asked him why he didn't say anything after I moved into the guestroom. We could've made other arrangements. I could have stayed at your grandparents."

"True. Why didn't you say something, John?" I asked.

"Because I kept thinking the problem would get better. When it didn't, I felt strong enough to stick it out until the wedding. Besides, I loved Jenny and didn't want to make her feel bad about what I was going through. When we were at school, I was handling my passions for her pretty well. But that all changed when we started living in the same house. I knew how much Jenny loved me and wanted to make me happy, and I was afraid that if I started complaining to her, she might be tempted to go against her convictions and offer to relieve my frustration. That would've been hard to say *no* to, and I couldn't chance messing up."

Jenny shared a few thoughts next. "My dad once told me that it wasn't a girl's responsibility to satisfy or manage a man's sexual needs while she was dating him. All men have sexual desires, and all men are supposed to control them. A guy who tries to push that responsibility off onto his girlfriend isn't much of a man.

"The girl's responsibility in a dating relationship is to make sure she's not being a tease, dressing immodestly, or pushing the limit physically. That's enticement, which is hard for most guys to resist. But if the man's having improper feelings toward her just because she's pretty, that's his problem. If he can't kiss her a few times without coming unglued, then he shouldn't kiss her. If he still has control problems or complains to her all the time, then the girl better not date him; he's trouble."

"That's right," John agreed. "Today I told you about some of my struggles before marrying Jenny. I wanted to show you that a man who truly loves you will sacrifice for you the way Christ did for the Church. And that's the best kind of man, Julia. Didn't Dad talk with you about jerks to watch out for at college?"

I thought for a few seconds. "Not that I can remember."

"You know, sis, I meant it when I asked you to forgive me earlier. Actually, both Dad and I are partly to blame for what happened. We never warned you about men like Jay. No wonder you fell for his lies. Didn't Dad tell you *anything* before going to school?"

"Sure he did. He told me to plug into a good church right away and find some Christian friends to hang out with."

"That was good advice, and you pretty much did that. Your mistake was hiding what you were doing from Mom and Dad, not discussing decisions and plans with them first. When you started doing that, you moved out from under their protection and into dangerous territory."

"You're right," I conceded.

"I hope you've learned your lesson and aren't hiding anything from them now. You aren't, are you?"

Instantly, I thought of the pictures and note from Jay.

"Julia, you're not answering," John sang out, suspiciously.

"Well, there is one little thing..."

"Like what?"

"The day before you and Jenny came home, I found an envelope in one of my textbooks. Inside were some pictures of Jay and me taken the night of the dance. There was also a note from him saying we'd eventually get married."

"I take it you didn't show any of this to Mom or Dad."

"No," I confessed.

"Where are those things now?"

"In my nightstand at home."

"Sounds like you plan to keep them."

"Ah...no, I'm going to throw them away."

"When?"

"Soon."

"How soon?"

"Hey, why are you grilling me?"

"Why are *you* hiding that stuff? Don't you see that you're making the same mistake again?"

"Well, honestly, I was worried about how Dad would react to seeing it. I didn't want to upset him, knowing how he feels about Jay."

"Trust me, Julia; Mom and Dad would rather have you tell them the truth, even if it upsets them a little. You just said honestly, so let's be honest. You're just using our parents' feelings as an excuse to keep that junk. You need to ask yourself why you would even want anything that reminds you of Jay."

"I don't know why, but for some reason, I don't want to throw them away yet," I admitted, looking down.

"Well, you don't have to understand why—just make yourself do it."

"Okay. I promise I will when I get back home."

"Good. But first you need to show them to Dad and Mom and admit when you found them. And to help you keep your promise, I'm going to email Dad a week after vacation and ask if you've talked with him."

"All right, John. I guess I owe it to Mom and Dad to be honest with them," I sighed, looking back up at him.

"I'm glad you see that, Julia. Are you relieved to finally have everything out in the open?"

"I am," I said, realizing that I *did* feel like a weight had been lifted. "Thanks, John."

"I don't know about you two," Jenny suddenly interrupted, "but I'm melting in this heat. Let's get in the water."

More than ready, we all stripped down to our bathing suits and enjoyed a relaxing swim in the pool below the falls. After an hour or so, John suggested we pack up and head back to the cottage. He was getting hungry and remembered that our grandmother still had more fish to fry for supper.

Prince or Pauper?

I loved early mornings at the cottage. Snugly wrapped in the blanket I had pulled off my bed, I sat alone on the front porch glider, enjoying the quiet. Watching the river flow slowly in the distance, I wondered if this was how it felt to sit in the Garden of Eden before daylight.

"Want some company?" a hushed voice unexpectedly asked, startling me. I turned to see Jenny poking her head around the screen door, shivering in her pajamas. "Brrr! It's kind of chilly out here, isn't it?"

"Get under," I invited, sitting up and extending half of the blanket to her.

Jenny didn't waste any time. She tiptoed across the wooden floor in her bare feet and hopped onto the glider, quickly tucking the blanket around her. "Ah... that's better," she sighed.

"What got you up so early?" I asked.

"Too much coffee after dinner, I guess. I've been tossing and turning for hours. What's your excuse?"

"I always come out here and watch the sun rise at least once while I'm at the cottage."

"I can see why. This place is beautiful. So, what are you drinking?" Jenny asked, looking at my cup longingly.

"Hot tea. I made a whole pot, but it's still on the stove."

"Be back in a second," Jenny said as she flipped off the blanket and jetted inside. Returning a few minutes later, she had a steaming mug of her own in one hand, the teapot in the other. "Want a refill?" she offered.

I lifted my mug. After pouring the tea, Jenny placed the pot on the side table next to the glider and squirmed under the blanket again, carefully balancing her cup to avoid a spill. Once she was settled, we chatted for a while and watched as the sun rose over the wooded horizon.

After a few more minutes of small talk, Jenny glanced over at me and asked, "Are you doing all right? It's been days since John and I talked with you at the cove, and I'm still seeing some of that lost look in your eyes."

"I'm not sure I'm feeling lost as much as I'm feeling alone," I answered. "Think about it, Jen. There are seven people in this house, and everyone has a special someone except me. It's hard not to feel out of place when everybody else is paired up. The worst part is that as much as I want to have a boyfriend,

I'm really not ready yet. I guess I'm a little jealous of where you and John are in life and what you have together."

"I wish there was a way I could speed up the waiting for you, Julia, but I can't. Just try to remember that the rest of us had to wait to get where we are now. We didn't always like it either, but because we trusted God and didn't get in a hurry, we each ended up fulfilled and married to the right person.

"Please don't take this wrong, Julia, but I think someone needs to say it. If you keep feeling sorry for yourself and go around unhappy most of the time, people won't like being around you. You'll make them feel uncomfortable. It's nobody's fault you're not ready for marriage yet, so don't make your family and friends feel guilty because they are. If you'll be happy for others now, they'll be happy for you later. Look at the good examples of the couples around you and be encouraged, knowing God is planning the same thing for you."

My eyes began to well up as I admitted, "You're right, Jenny. Only I don't know how to be happy while I wait. Do I just act happy when I'm really not?"

"You might have to start out that way, Julia. We all have feelings; we just have to make a conscious decision to manage them. When you decide to be a happy person and act that way, in time your feelings will catch up with you. My mom used to tell the young women of our church who were frustrated with waiting that they needed to stop watching the clock. Then she would explain with a simple story."

Jenny shifted to a more comfortable position on the glider and then continued:

There once was a woman who had a date with her dream man. Excited, she came home early from work and started getting ready right away. Even though she knew he wouldn't be at her house until eight, she was fully dressed by five and sat down on the couch to watch the clock while she waited. It seemed like an eternity for those three hours to pass before he finally arrived.

There were plenty of other things she could've been doing while she was waiting. Her younger sister was having trouble with her math homework, and her mother would've appreciated some help making dinner. Likewise, her father was finishing a project in the garage and would have welcomed the input of his daughter.

But because the woman was so focused on herself, she was blind to the needs of the people around her—all the while professing to love them. She still had to wait the three hours for her date to show up; that didn't change. But no one else got blessed while she was waiting, and she was anxious and frustrated the whole time.

"That's a great analogy, Jen," I commented when she finished. "It's easy to only think of yourself when you're waiting for something you really want. You were close to your mom, weren't you?"

Now Jenny had tears in her eyes. "Very close. When she died in that car accident, I was devastated. I'd lost my mom at a difficult time, just as I was finishing high school and trying to decide where to study nursing. I had always talked to my mom about everything and I missed her so much. I knew she was safe in heaven, but it was still hard to be without her.

"Eventually, I was able to see past myself to my dad's pain. My parents had been happily married for thirty years, and he was lost without her. Seeing the lost look in your eyes this week reminded me of the one I often saw in his.

"So really, Julia, there are lots of people in this world who are *not* paired up. Many have had mates and then lost them for some reason. Maybe they got divorced or their spouse died or left them. They're dealing with the same void of being alone, but their pain is probably greater after knowing what it's like to be in an intimate relationship and then having to live without it."

"I guess I'm a lot like Amy with her glasses," I mused, thinking of a comparison.

Jenny looked baffled. "Huh? I don't get it."

I tried to explain. "My mom had a friend in school named Amy. She was fun, smart, and always surrounded by friends, but she didn't feel good about herself because she wore glasses. When she finally started wearing contact lenses, she realized there were people all around her wearing glasses. She'd never noticed that before. Her insecurity about wearing them had made her focus only on herself.

"To be honest, Jen, I've been doing a lot of focusing on myself lately. I'm really self-conscious because I don't have a boyfriend. Even though I understand all the reasons why I'm waiting for the right guy, others don't. When I get back to school in the fall, people might think something's wrong with me because I don't have a boyfriend."

"Let them, Julia. It's a waste of time worrying about the opinions of others, especially when those people don't even care about you. Look around and you'll see lots of girls who aren't dating anyone. Remember, you can always find *somebody* to go out with—especially if you're willing to give him whatever he wants. The question is: do you want a prince or a pauper?"

"A prince, of course! But I'm not sure what you're getting at."

"Okay, let me explain what I mean. When I was growing up, life was a little different for me, Julia. My dad was a pastor, so I was labeled a *pk*, which stands for *pastor's kid*. Because a pastor's family is supposed to be an example to the congregation, people tend to expect more from them than from the average Christian. So that meant my behavior was constantly being scrutinized, or at least that's how I felt.

"I was considered a pretty girl, and lots of times I'd get attention from guys who thought that dating the pastor's daughter would make them look important at church. It was more about impressing other people than liking me for who I was. Worse than that, some of the non-Christian guys at my school saw a pastor's daughter as a challenge and asked me out just to try to get me to do something wrong.

"My parents understood all those pressures and temptations and kept a close eye on my social life. I was allowed to hang out with my church friends and go to lots of different Christian events, but sometimes I felt like I was being overprotected.

"When I told my mom I was feeling that way, she said that my friends and activities as a teenager would have a lot to do with the person I'd become and the man I'd someday marry. Then she asked me if I wanted to end up with a prince or a pauper. When I looked confused, she went to my room and pulled out a book of fairy tales from one of my shelves. Then we sat down together and talked for a while." Jenny paused for a moment to set her empty mug down on the side table. Turning back to me, she relayed the conversation:

"Do you remember this story?" my mom asked, opening the book to the Cinderella tale by the French author, Charles Perrault.

"Sure," I answered. "Every girl knows that one."

"Yes, but does every girl understand the meaning behind it? There are some truths here you might find interesting. First of all, Cinderella is portrayed through most of the story as a maid constantly mistreated by her stepmother and stepsisters. Her life is so oppressed, you begin to think of her as an actual peasant girl. But that wasn't the case. Actually, Cinderella's father was a man of position and wealth in the kingdom and her mother, a lady of high breeding and character.

"As you know, when Cinderella's mother died, her father remarried a woman who was bad-tempered and haughty. She had two daughters of her own who, although they were attractive, were just as hateful as their mother. Because Cinderella was incredibly beautiful and good-natured, all three of them were jealous and treated her cruelly, as a servant in her own home.

"But to Cinderella's credit, no matter how ragged she appeared or how unfairly she was treated, her beautiful countenance and kind heart were untouched. She served her family to the best of her ability without complaining, and she never displayed any malicious feelings toward them.

"Now, any change in Cinderella's situation was beyond hope in the natural. Only a miracle could save her from living life as a peasant and one day marrying a pauper. As we know, a miracle did happen. Cinderella's fairy godmother gave her a beautiful gown and coach to go to the kingdom ball two nights in a row. There the prince saw Cinderella and fell in love with her instantly. But the fairy's transformation only lasted until midnight, so each night Cinderella was forced to leave before the clock struck twelve.

"You know the rest of the story. On the second night, Cinderella lost her glass slipper, the prince used it to find her, and the two were married soon after at the royal palace. The author doesn't tell us what happened after that. We're just left to assume they lived happily ever after. So, let me ask you a question, Jenny. What enabled Cinderella to enjoy a lasting and happy marriage with her prince? She barely knew him when they got married."

Unsure, I simply shrugged I didn't know.

My mother smiled before she went on. "The answer is: Cinderella had already developed the heart of a princess, so she was ready to sit beside her husband on the throne when the time came.

"You see, Jen, every Christian girl is like Cinderella. You are all daughters of the King of the Universe and are entitled to marry a prince, have a royal wedding, and enjoy a happy life. But there is an enemy at work to keep you from meeting and marrying your prince, and he'll use whatever diversions he can to get you off course.

"Of course, we know fairy godmothers don't exist. But if you continue to trust God, the Holy Spirit will provide whatever supernatural help you need to get to *your* appointed destiny. And it's important for you to start developing the character of a princess now, before you even meet your prince.

"Now, before you get carried away with this story and start thinking that your prince has to be rich and famous, we'd better back up and define who a prince is in the eyes of God. He is first a son of the King, someone who has made Jesus Christ his Savior and Lord.

"The *Lord* part is important, Jenny. A lot of people call Jesus their Savior, but they don't honor God with the way they live their lives. When Jesus is your *Lord*, you seek His will for your life and do your best to follow what God tells you to do in the Bible.

"So a prince is a man who submits himself to God and lives his life with integrity. He also must be able to handle responsibility. When a man reaches this level of maturity, God can help him love his wife sacrificially and raise his children to follow Christ.

"Some men are called to ministry life, like your dad, while others pursue white collar professions or blue collar jobs. The Lord will bless every man who puts his trust in Him and earns an honest living. He will give him everything he needs for his family, plus something extra to help and bless others.

"Jenny, God will match you up with a man you can help in life. He will have a specific calling from God, and you will share in that calling. The qualities you need to be a faithful wife are already within you, Jen. Since you want to be married someday, focus on

developing your gifts and talents as you trust God to bring you together with your mate, when and where the time is right.

"Waiting for a husband doesn't mean sitting around aimlessly. It means moving forward, growing, learning, and enjoying life until that season comes. But remember, once you're married, your personal ambitions must work in harmony with your relationship with your husband and the raising of your children. You were designed by God to be his helpmate—not the other way around.

"If you interfere with God's timing or try to redesign His system, you could miss out on meeting your prince and end up with a pauper. A pauper isn't necessarily a man who hasn't achieved anything in life by the world's standards; he's simply a man who has little to offer you because he's spiritually bankrupt."

Amazed by the way Jenny's mother interpreted the Cinderella story, I blurted out, "Wow, that's good. I wish I had known your mom, Jen. She had a lot of wisdom."

"Thanks. The day after our talk, she gave me a journal and asked me to write *Getting to Know God* on the inside cover. Then she told me to do something that surprised me."

"Really? What?"

"She told me to start writing out prayers to God and to also start praying for my husband, even though

I had no idea who he was." Jenny immediately went on to share her mom's advice:

> "The man God has chosen for you is somewhere out there already, Jen. He may still be in high school like you, or maybe he's in college by now.
>
> "The next few years are going to be filled with a lot of pressure for him. He's expected to someday earn a living for his family, so he's choosing a career and preparing for it right now. Depending upon how long he goes to school, he could be well into his twenties before he meets and marries you.
>
> "This means that as a Christian man, he must refrain from sexual activity during the years when his sex drive is the strongest. Some women don't understand how much mental and physical anguish a man suffers during his premarital years. It takes a spirit-controlled man to successfully manage his passions during this time in his life.
>
> "Take this journal and write down a list of the things you want in a husband. Don't focus on physical traits, like his height or the color of his hair. If you do, you might create a wrong image that keeps you from recognizing him when he does come into your life—all because he doesn't match the picture you've formed in your mind. Trust God. He'll make sure that

your guy's attractive to you, just as you'll be to him.

"Instead, concentrate on all the *character* traits you're trusting God to develop in your future husband, like being a good communicator or somebody who cares about other people. Maybe someone who is fun to be around and makes you laugh. Then write down what God needs to develop in you to be a good wife for him.

"Start to pray for him in areas where he needs God's help. Pray for things like his spiritual growth, his schooling, the friends he's choosing, the girls who are trying to tempt him, and his finances. Your prayers may help him in the middle of an important decision or simply bring encouragement when he needs it most.

"Remember, you'll be living and working alongside this man for the rest of your life. He's worth the time you invest now praying for him. Hopefully, he's praying for you, too. Try to understand that while you're going through some suffering by having to wait for your young man, he's most likely going through just as much frustration—as well as fighting a lot of mental and physical temptation.

"Scripture teaches us that God doesn't bring confusion. He watches His sons and daughters and knows when they are submitted to Him and mature enough to be a good marriage partner. The Lord will not bring a man into your life who makes you miserable with his immaturity or rebellion. And vice versa.

"Remember, Jenny: while a girl may be anxious to be a bride, she may not be ready to become a wife. After a wedding comes a marriage and all the responsibilities that go with it. Even an elaborate wedding only lasts a day, but a marriage is designed by God to last a lifetime."

Jenny looked a little sad when she recalled, "That was the last serious talk I had with my mom before her accident. I never expected to know a mother's love again after I lost her, but God brought me into your family. Your mom has really been there for me, Julia. Cherish her. She's full of godly wisdom, too, you know."

"I know. We had some great talks before I came home from school, and I was reminded just how blessed I am to have her. Actually, our whole family's great. I keep thinking about how today's the last time we'll see you and John before you leave for Chile. We're going to miss you so much. Three years seems like forever. Make sure you guys keep in touch."

At that moment, muffled voices could be heard in the background, signaling that the rest of the family was awake. Jenny turned and looked back inside the cottage. "I guess I'll go see if John's up."

"Thanks for talking with me, Jen. A lot of what you said helped. I think I'll start writing in a journal when I get home."

"Good. Mine still helps me to stay focused and develop my relationship with God."

"That's my first priority now," I replied as we both got up to go inside. "I want to make the Lord my first love."

Jenny smiled as we gathered up our things. "It's been fun hanging out again this week. I never had a sister to talk to before I married John."

I managed to free up one hand and put my arm around Jenny's shoulder as we squeezed through the entrance of the cottage. "I love having you for a sister, too."

Chapter 4

Beauty Lessons

A loud clap of thunder awakened me from a sound sleep. At first, I couldn't remember where I was. Looking around, I realized I was home in my own bed and it was Thursday—the day I had decided to show my parents Jay's note and pictures hidden in my nightstand. We had been back from the cottage for almost a week, and I didn't dare postpone my confession any longer, not knowing when John would be emailing our dad to confirm I'd kept our agreement.

With a yawn, I raised my head and looked over at the alarm clock. It was almost nine a.m. The sound of the rain pelting against the windows tempted me to turn over and go back to sleep, but I remembered that Cassie was coming over at ten-thirty, forcing me to get up and into the shower.

After dressing and straightening up my room, I went down to the kitchen to get something to eat.

Both of my parents were already at the office, and it was the housekeeper's day off. I had the place all to myself. Checking the refrigerator, I found some left-over pizza and quickly popped it into the microwave. Knowing that wasn't the healthiest breakfast, I also grabbed a banana off the counter and poured myself a glass of milk.

As I sat and ate, I mentally rehearsed what I was going to say to my parents at dinner. Why was I making this such a big deal? I would just show the envelope to them and say I found it in one of my books. I wouldn't have to mention *when* I found it. That way I could toss everything into the trash in front of them, and nobody would get upset.

Then I remembered that John's email would reveal that I'd found the note and pictures sometime *before* we went to the cottage. My brother's words replayed in my mind: "Don't you see that you're making the same mistake again?"

John was right. I had to tell my parents the truth. And the truth was I'd been hiding those things from them. Maybe someday I would understand why, but for now, just like John said, the important thing was to simply confess and get rid of my contraband.

Sighing, I began to pray. *"I'm beginning to see a dangerous pattern in my life, Lord. When I do some-thing wrong, I instinctively try to hide my mistake so I won't have to admit my weakness or failure. Then, even worse, I rationalize it by saying I don't want to hurt or upset others. Really, I'm just trying to protect myself..."*

Just then the doorbell rang, cutting off my prayer. Jumping up from the table, I rinsed my dirty dish in the sink and sprinted toward the foyer. I fully expected to see Cassie when I opened the door, but I was surprised to find her standing on the stoop, dripping wet.

"You sure took your time getting here!" Cassie complained as she quickly stepped into the house and planted herself on the large circular rug in the foyer.

"Sorry, I was just finishing breakfast," I laughed. Quickly, I went and fetched a towel for my guest. Extending it toward her, I remarked, "It's been pouring rain all morning, Cass. When are you going to learn to keep an umbrella in your car?"

"I get tired of buying umbrellas and then leaving them everywhere I go," Cassie answered with a grin, wrapping the towel around her shoulders. "Besides, it's a good excuse to borrow an outfit from you. I'm soaked. Got something I can wear?"

"You know I do. If you're through dripping all over the place, let's go upstairs and find something."

Feeling right at home, Cassie followed me into my bedroom and headed straight to my walk-in closet. Grabbing a shirt and some jeans, she quickly changed into dry clothes.

"Lucky we're the same size," I pointed out from where I had flopped down on the bed.

"Luck has nothing to do with it," Cassie announced, coming out of the closet. "With my metabolism and three good workouts a week, I should be able to fit

into your clothes for life. That's if *you* stay the same size through the years, of course."

"Well, I'll try. Just for you. But what if after we get married, we don't live close enough for you to borrow my clothes anymore?"

"I'm not worried. By that time, I'll have a husband to buy me all the clothes I need. And I won't have to go looking all over the house for a missing skirt or sweater because one of my sisters is already wearing it!"

I laughed. There were times I wished I *did* have that problem. Sisters could be pests sometimes, but they were also a lot of fun. Cassie pulled my desk chair up close to the bed and sat down. Taking a pick out of her purse, she began running it through her wet hair. "So, what's up? You said to come over this morning so you could tell me something."

"Actually, it's something I want to show you," I said, reaching into my nightstand drawer. I pulled out the envelope and held it out to Cassie. "I found this in one of my books a few weeks ago. Jay must have stuffed it in there while we were at the library the day after the dance. Probably right after I told him we couldn't see each other anymore."

Cassie took the envelope from me and opened it. After leafing through the pictures, she unfolded the note and read it. "So this is the jerk," she murmured, reviewing the pictures a second time.

"That's him. What do you think?"

Cassie looked up at me. "I just told you what I think. He's a jerk. What did you expect?"

"Well, I guess I expected you to say how good-looking he is."

"Okay, he's good looking. But I've got to tell you, Julia, I already had that figured out befo   re seeing these pictures. There had to be some reason you stayed with him so long. After what he did to you, isn't looking at these kind of disturbing?"

"Yes, but for some reason, I haven't been able to throw them away. I can't really explain why. I guess I wanted you to see what Jay looked like before I got rid of them."

"What were you hoping I'd say? That nobody could've resisted this guy, not even me?"

"That's what I love about you, Cass; you just tell it like it is. I hate to admit it, but you're probably right. Maybe I'm still looking for a way to justify what I did. You know, find a reason for being so stupid."

"Will you please stop apologizing for being human? You trusted the guy, and he turned out to be a phony. It happens. Your biggest mistake was hiding your relationship with Jay from people you already knew you could trust. You could've told me, Julia. I am your best friend, you know."

"I know," I answered, cringing. "Sorry I wasn't honest with you. I guess I knew what you'd say if I told you, and I didn't want to hear it. It's funny. I always wanted to have a boyfriend, but never had one until Jay. You have a guy who's been crazy about you since eighth grade, yet you've always kept your relationship with Brian as just friends. I've known for years that you like him as more than that, even though you won't admit it. Come on, fess up. Why haven't you told him? All he's waiting for is some sign that you like him, too."

"All right, I *do* care for Brian. He's a great guy and everything I want in a boyfriend. But he's always wanted to be a lawyer, and that means he's got to get through college *and* law school. If I'd encouraged Brian from the time he started liking me, what would we have done as our feelings for each other grew? How long do you think two people can be together without wanting to express their love sexually? As Christians, we'd have to get married to do that. We both still have years of school to finish before marriage is even a possibility."

"But what if Brian gets tired of waiting and falls for someone else?"

"Then he isn't the man God has for me. I want to get married someday just as much as you do, Julia, but I'm not in any hurry. Believe me; I know all about being a wife and mother. We've been best friends since we were girls, but we've lived really different lives. Coming from a family of seven, do you know what marriage means to me? It means washing, cooking, cleaning, taking care of babies, and no privacy!"

"I've been to your place millions of times, Cass, and I haven't noticed that much difference between your family and mine, except for maybe having more kids around."

"I didn't say our *families* were all that different. We both come from homes with good Christian parents where we've been happy and loved all our lives. I'm just pointing out that our *lives at home* were different. Not necessarily better or worse, just different.

"Face it, Julia. Your dad makes a lot more money than mine, and we've never had a maid like Kitty. At our house, we all have to work together as a family to get everything done. I love spending time here because it's like leaving the real world for a while and stepping into a fantasyland where everything's beautiful and easy."

"That's funny, Cassie, because in a lot of ways, I've always envied you."

"You're kidding, right?"

"No, I'm not. You truly enjoy life—even when everything's not perfect. Then there's me. I seem to always be working through some emotional crisis. It makes me feel like there's something wrong with me."

"There's nothing wrong with you, Julia. You've been the most giving friend I've ever had. As I see it, your parents just made the mistake of protecting you too much. So when you came face to face with a Mr. Wrong, you weren't able to see through his lies."

"Maybe that was my problem. Be honest, Cass. You wouldn't have been fooled by Jay the way I was, would you?"

"I don't know, maybe not since I already know the world's full of jerks. You just had to learn it the hard way." Pausing to glance at her watch, she sighed. "I'd better get going. I have to watch my brother so my mom can do some shopping. Walk me to the door, will you?"

Nodding, I sat up and rolled off the bed where I'd been reclining during our talk. As we made our way downstairs, I put my arm around Cassie and said, "Pray for me tonight. I have to tell my parents that I found Jay's note and pictures a couple weeks ago, that I've sort of been hiding them in my room."

"Sort of?"

"Okay, I've been purposely hiding them. I told John about them at the cove, and he made me promise to show everything to Mom and Dad when I got home. I'm going to do it after dinner."

"Why didn't you just show them that stuff right away?"

"To tell you the truth, I knew my dad would make me get rid of it, and I didn't want to. True confessions: I look at those pictures a few times a day."

"Knowing what Jay did to you, I'm not even going to try to figure that one out. I'm just going to pray that God shows you why Jay still has this much of a hold on you. You may need to have someone in authority, like your parents or Pastor Mark, pray for you and break that emotional tie."

"That's not a bad idea. I'll call you tomorrow and tell you how everything went."

"Hey, the sun's out," Cassie remarked as she stepped out the door and walked to her car. "Phone me before lunch," she called out before getting in. "I'm going shopping with my mom around twelve-thirty. My wet clothes are in your closet. I'll get them when I bring your shirt and jeans back."

Once Cassie was gone, I hopped in my car and drove downtown to buy a journal. I promised myself at the cottage that when I got home, I would spend time with the Lord every day. After my conversation with Jenny, I was more excited than ever to begin journaling and start praying for my future husband.

After looking in several stores, I finally found the right journal. When I got back home, I wrote *Getting to Know God* on the inside cover, just like Jenny had done in hers years before.

Next, I studied Proverbs 31, verses 10-31 in my Bible. Those scriptures touched my heart, and I wrote my first journal entry as a prayer:

Father,

I can see that the Proverbs 31 woman is a standard, a model for women of every age. I want to be like her. Although she kept herself beautiful for her husband and family, her greatest attribute was her godly character.

Vanity is one of my biggest problems, Lord. I don't like to admit it, but it's true. As I look back on my experience with Jay, I'm sure I gave in to his charm because he was so handsome and he made me feel pretty. I did enjoy showing him off to my friends as if to say, "Look what I've got!" I didn't realize it at the time.

Women sometimes accuse men of treating them like trophies, just something to show off to the other guys. Was I any less self-centered and shallow with Jay?

Now that I see vanity as one of my flaws, I ask You to forgive me and help me to change. I know I can't do it by myself, but Your Word says I can do anything when You strengthen me. Father, by faith, I believe You've heard my prayer and that from this moment on, I'll improve in this area of my life. I ask this in the name of Jesus.

I had just spent an hour with my Heavenly Father studying and praying, but it seemed like only a few minutes. Writing in my journal, I'd entered into a closeness with God I hadn't experienced before. In fact, I'd become so lost in His presence, it was hard to break away when my mom called that dinner was ready.

Closing my journal, I got up from the desk, walked to my nightstand, and took out the envelope I'd been hiding. Then I stuffed it into the back pocket of my jeans and went downstairs.

Dinner seemed to take forever as I worked up the courage to make my confession. Finally, just as my parents were about to leave the table, I pulled out the envelope and told them everything. Much to my surprise, they weren't upset at all when they looked at the pictures and read Jay's note. They just wanted to know why I hid it all from them.

I took a deep breath before answering. "At first I thought it was because I didn't want Dad to get mad. The truth is I was afraid he'd make me throw it all away. It's hard to explain, but when I was dating Jay, I felt special in a way I'd never known before. I kept the note and pictures because they remind me of when a handsome guy like Jay thought I was beautiful."

My mom smiled and asked me an unexpected question. "So, if Jay *hadn't* found you beautiful, would that have meant you weren't?"

Pondering her question for a moment, I said, "I'm not sure how to answer you."

"That's because you still need to learn what true beauty is, Julia. Physical beauty gets a lot of attention in our culture, but that kind of beauty has little value, mainly because it's both subjective and fading. One man can look at a girl and think she's pretty, while another might not find her attractive at all. The girl's appearance is not the variable—just the opinions of her observers. This will be true for her as long as she lives. And as the years pass, physical beauty fades. That's Scriptural."

"I just read that today in Proverbs 31," I interrupted. "It says that, 'Charm is deceptive, and beauty does not last; but a woman who fears the Lord will be greatly praised.'"

"Exactly. I like what it says in verse 25 of the *Living Bible*." My mom reached behind her and grabbed her copy, which was conveniently lying on the corner of the buffet table. Flipping through the pages, she found that passage and read it. "'She is a woman of strength and dignity, and has no fear of old age.'

"The beauty that's most worth developing, Julia, is the beauty of a godly character. That doesn't mean we neglect our personal appearance. The woman of Proverbs 31 certainly didn't. I'm just saying that it's the good person God helps us to become, the kind words we speak, and things we do for others that endear us to people and make us truly beautiful and worthy in their eyes.

"You said that Jay made you *feel* special. You must remember that feelings are fickle, sweetheart. They change like the weather. You probably felt pretty and special because Jay complimented you and paid you a lot of attention. But if you believe your beauty as a woman is dependent on a man's evaluation of you, you're giving that man a lot of manipulative power over you. What will happen if you see he's not as attentive to you as he used to be? Will you no longer feel beautiful and try to perform somehow to get his interest back?

"If a man should lose interest in you over time before you're married, that only means he's unstable himself or God didn't intend for your relationship to be permanent. That's no reflection on you; you're still the same.

"Sometimes feelings of not being beautiful are nothing more than that—feelings. Maybe you're overtired or having an *I feel ugly* day, for who-knows-what reason. But if you're confident in your heart that you are a beautiful woman, the enemy won't be able to use the opinions of others or your own unpredictable feelings to rob you of your dignity and worth.

"I don't know if you realize it, Julia, but in God's eyes, every woman is beautiful, valuable, and desirable. I have known many women who have understood that, and although the world wouldn't classify them as rare beauties, they have attracted, married, and enjoyed lasting relationships with some very good-looking and successful men."

"I know that to be true," my dad volunteered. "My friend in law school had a girlfriend named Carla. When I first met her, I thought she was on the plain side. But it wasn't long before I started to see her differently. There was something about her that was really likeable. She had a quick wit, great smile, and was fun to be around. She was really interesting to talk to and genuinely cared about what you had to say. Eventually, the beautiful person she was on the inside began to affect the way you saw her on the outside. Carla carried herself well, had a nice wardrobe, and wore her hair and makeup attractively. You could say she knew how to make the most of what she had. When she and Bob got married, there were quite a few men at that wedding who were jealous."

"I knew an absolutely *gorgeous* girl in school," my mom added, "who didn't have such a happy life. Her name was Carrie, and she was popular with guys from the time she was in junior high. With her beautiful face and figure, she always had a boyfriend, went to every social event, and had tons of friends. It was hard not to envy her.

"We didn't keep in touch after graduation, but about fifteen years later, I ran into a friend who had seen her while traveling on business. Carrie was eating at the same restaurant, and she recognized Linda right away and started a conversation. Finally,

Linda had to admit that she couldn't remember her name.

"When the woman told her who she was, Linda couldn't believe it. The glamour girl we had known in high school had her hair pulled back into a bun, wore absolutely no makeup, and was dressed very drably.

"Reading the shocked look on Linda's face, Carrie admitted she had changed a lot. Then she went on to explain that she'd been through two bad marriages and several unhappy relationships since high school. Tired of being admired and sought after merely for her looks, Carrie had completely changed her image.

"She found that she was finally able to work without being sexually harassed by the men in the office and had developed some genuine friends for the first time in her life. She finally felt appreciated for the intelligent and capable person she had always been.

"Although Carrie's self-made solution was an overreaction to her problem, it proves something important, Julia. Each of us wants to be loved and appreciated for who we are as a person instead of how we look. It also proves that we'll do just about anything we can in order to find that kind of acceptance."

My dad saw a break in the conversation and immediately took advantage of it. "If the beauty lessons are over, there's something I need to tell you two."

No More Secrets

With our undivided attention, my dad continued. "First, I need to admit that the contents of your envelope, my darling daughter, were not a surprise to me tonight. I already knew about them."

Both my mom and I looked at him, puzzled. Reading our expressions, he immediately explained. "Remember the phone call I decided to take in my study last night? You two thought it was from a client, but it wasn't. The call was from John.

"He had fully intended to email me this week as per your agreement with him at the cove, but when he was praying about it, he felt he should talk to me directly. I'm grateful we had that talk, ladies. I didn't like some of the things he had to say, but I definitely needed to hear them.

"When you got into your mess at school, Julia, I really wasn't all that surprised you were taken in by a smooth talker like Jay. Men like that can be deceiving. What really bothered me was the way you kept your relationship with him a secret from us—that you were deliberately dishonest about something so important. I've asked myself over and over why you would hide the truth from me, why you weren't able to trust my love for you. I got my answer last night when I talked to John. The answer is *because you're just like your father.*"

I didn't know how to react to that statement, but my mom responded with a smile that implied *I already know what you're about to say.*

My dad didn't wait for me to respond. He simply went on. "Actually, Julia, we're *both* good at hiding things. For years, I've been keeping something about my father and me a secret. I always thought my reasons were in your best interest, but in reality, my motives were more about protecting myself. Sound familiar?"

I shook my head *yes.*

My dad took a few sips of his coffee before he was ready to tell all. "From the moment we brought you home, Julia, you were our little princess, and we did everything in our power to make you happy, to protect you. By the time you were old enough to understand about my father and me, I didn't have the heart to tell you. Your grandpa had already died by then, and I figured it was pointless to ruin your good opinion of him.

"The truth is, Julia, your grandfather wasn't a good man, and I was ashamed of him. You've always looked up to me as your dad, and I didn't want to admit to you how much I'd hated my father. But after talking with John last night, I can see it's time I finally explained it to you."

I was speechless. Scooting my chair up to the table, I leaned in closer, anxious to hear the whole story. My imagination was off and running.

Taking a final sip of his coffee, my dad leaned back in his chair and began:

My dad was born into a wealthy family out East. Unfortunately, his father was totally consumed by business and had no time for his family. My dad spent all his life trying to gain the approval of his father, never succeeding. In fact, when my dad returned home from college, his father told him point blank that he meant nothing to him, that he would never amount to anything. My dad was crushed. Angry and resentful, he vowed to prove his father wrong. He immediately applied to law school and eventually graduated at the top of his class.

A few months later, he met your grandmother, and they were married shortly after he started practicing law. But even her love couldn't make up for his father's total rejection of him.

Instead, he began to drink excessively, and his bitterness drove him even deeper into his work. He took on the most difficult cases, not caring what he had to do to win. He was known for being ruthless and unethical, his hatred for his

father was gradually turning him into a cruel and uncaring person.

Sad to say, at home my dad was no better than his father had been. He was a tyrant with my mother and virtually ignored both your aunt and me. After dinner, he would go to his study and drink himself to sleep.

I grew up greatly fearing and resenting my dad, Julia. You might wonder why I wanted to become a lawyer like my father. Actually, it had nothing to do with him. I just loved courtrooms and the whole legal process.

As you know, I was still in law school when I met your mother. I was visiting my sister at Weston U, and we decided to go to a Christian conference on campus that Friday night. When she introduced me to your mom, I lost my heart in an instant.

I invited her out for dinner the next night so we could get to know each other before I had to leave. We had a great time, and when I brought her home, I asked if I could drive up on the weekends to see her. I was thrilled when she said yes.

We've shared part of the story of our courtship, Julia, but some things you don't know—like the fact that our first date was our last one for almost a year and a half.

Here's the whole truth. I wanted to see your mom one more time before leaving town, so I showed up at her church in the morning with my sister, and we all sat together during the service.

When it was over, Grandpa Carl said that he and I should walk downtown and get a sandwich, that he wanted to talk with me privately. His tone of voice told me I'd better accept his invitation, so I said a quick goodbye to your mom, and she and your aunt went home with Grandma.

That walk downtown was the longest of my life. Your grandfather didn't look angry, but he wasn't overly friendly either. I kept asking myself what I had done wrong. I'd been a perfect gentleman with his daughter the night before, and I couldn't figure out what was going on.

Finally, we arrived at a small café and were seated at a table toward the back. Grandpa was pleasant enough during our meal, but it wasn't until we were finished eating that he was ready to tell me the reason for our lunch together. He started out by saying, "Son, it would seem we've got ourselves a situation here."

I sat there stunned for several seconds. No man had ever called me *son* before. I'd always longed to hear my dad call me that, but he never had. At last, I responded, "What kind of a situation?"

"The one with you and our Gracie," he answered, trying to make eye contact with me. "I saw the way you two looked at each other in church. Even though you've only had one date with her, there's obviously a strong attraction between you. I've got to put a stop to it before things go any further."

I sat there speechless, trying to sort through what he had said. Why was this man rejecting me without even knowing me? Finally, I had to ask him, "Sir, have I done something to offend you?"

"No, son. I'm sure that in many ways you're a fine young man. But I can tell that you're dealing with some rejection issues, and I don't want my daughter falling in love with a man who's emotionally wounded."

"Why do you think I'm wounded, Mr. Sanders?" I asked, surprised.

Grandpa smiled before he answered me. "From the moment we met, you've avoided eye contact with me, Phil. There's something wrong with a man who can't look me in the eye when I'm talking to him. He's either wounded inside or hiding something. I don't think you're hiding anything, son; I just think you've got a broken heart.

"Your sister and Grace have become close friends over the last few weeks. She's been at our home a lot and shared quite a bit about your family, especially about your dad.

"I've learned over the years how important a good father-son relationship is toward building a solid foundation in every man. I'm a contractor, and I know that a building can be beautiful from the ground up, but if the foundation's faulty, eventually the rest of the structure will have serious problems.

"The Bible teaches us that all the issues of life come out of our hearts. That means the heart is the foundation of every person. If you plan to have a healthy relationship with any woman, you'll need to get your heart fixed before you give it away to her. You'll never be all God wants you to be as a husband and father until you do."

Your grandfather was right, and I knew it. I did have resentment in my heart towards my dad, and I had missed out on any kind of positive male role modeling as a boy. I don't remember exactly what I said to Grandpa next, but I think it was something like, "So, how do I get my heart fixed, Mr. Sanders? I'm not a kid anymore; I'm a grown man."

"God isn't limited by age, Phil. He can fix the heart of anyone who's willing to surrender to Him. Are you willing?"

I stopped and thought for a moment. "What exactly are you proposing?"

"That you get with a positive role model and let him help fill the relational void you have in your heart—let him teach you to draw from God what you missed getting from your father growing up—to help you feel good about yourself so you'll have the confidence to look any man square in the eye when he's talking to you."

"Who would do that for me?" I asked.

"I would," he immediately offered. "But before you accept, you should know what I'll expect.

We need to spend a lot of time together, so you'll have to be here in Weston on most weekends and during your school breaks. I'll give you a job at the yard this summer, too. You won't be coming to my house, so don't agree to this thinking you'll see Grace often. That's not going to happen.

"This arrangement has nothing to do with your feelings for Grace. It's about building a right foundation in you as a man. From now on, I want you to focus on relating with me and the other godly men I plan to use. This will take commitment on your part, but if you'll stick with me until I'm done, you'll come out on the other side with a healthy self-image and a Christ-centered way of living. You'll be a man who knows how to fulfill his responsibilities to God, family, church, and community."

"How long do you think this will take?"

"That all depends on you, son. It could take weeks, months, or even years."

"How will I know when we're finished?"

Grandpa chuckled. "You won't know; I will. And when I see that you're where you need to be, we'll come back to this restaurant and have another talk. If you still want to date Gracie and she agrees, I'll give you permission to see her then."

I deeply wanted what your grandfather offered, so I agreed and we shook on it. He asked me to come the next weekend, and once he set me up

with a family to stay with in Weston, my training began.

The first thing your grandfather did was teach me how to forgive my father for failing me. He made me realize that bitterness and resentment were like poisons that would damage not only my soul, but also the lives of everyone around me. He said if I refused to forgive my dad, the next generation would be worse than the last—that the only way to reverse the curse in my family was to allow genuine forgiveness to heal my heart.

I knew he was right. My father was definitely worse than my grandfather had been, and I wanted to make sure that I wouldn't pass that curse down to my son someday.

Over the next eighteen months, I spent a lot of time with Grandpa. He taught me the importance of Bible study and prayer and had me working with him so much, I felt like his shadow. When he wasn't available, he teamed me up with other men on his crew. Although I wasn't a very good handyman, I loved working with those men. They gave me what I needed most: a real sense of acceptance. Looking back, I don't know how I spent so much time in Weston and still got through law school, but God gave me the grace to do it.

Grandpa was true to his word. When he felt I was ready, he took me to lunch at that same café and told me he was proud of the man I had become, that I had his permission to date his daughter.

Thinking my dad was finished, I immediately turned to my mom and blurted out, "So, how did you feel about all this? Were you still attracted to Dad that whole time?"

My mom winked at my dad and admitted, "I certainly was!"

"Did you ever get to see each other?"

"A little. We saw each other at church and at the singles' events. Sometimes we'd run into each other around town as well. To his credit, your dad honored your grandpa's wishes and never tried to meet me secretly. I think he was afraid of losing the chance to date me later."

"Were you mad at Grandpa for keeping you two apart?" I asked.

"No, not really. I knew your grandfather loved me and only wanted to protect me. Even though I was attracted to your father, I trusted my dad and didn't want to get involved with a man who had serious issues."

My dad broke into the conversation again. "Have you ever wondered why I didn't insist that you press charges against Jay? What he did was a criminal offense, you know."

"I guess I never thought about it," I answered.

"There was a reason why, Julia. Remember when I left your hospital room to tell Jay you were awake and out of danger?"

"Yes, I asked you not to be too rough on him."

"That's right. Well, I never told you what happened when he heard you were going to be okay. He broke down and cried like a baby. He kept saying how sorry he was, that he never meant to hurt you, that all he wanted was for you two to get married. Because of what he'd done, I told him he wasn't to see or contact you again. Period. He seemed to understand my decision, but he was heartbroken.

"He confided in me about his parents and the way they had rejected him all his life. He thought your love would make up for his past. My anger toward him lessened because I knew just how he felt, with one exception. Although my dad never showed any interest in me, I at least had a godly mother who loved me. Jay hadn't known the love of either of his parents.

"I shared with him what I'd gone through with my dad, and he seemed interested in my story. I pointed out that the most important relationship in his life would not be with a woman, but with Christ, who created him and gave His life to save him. I said that no woman could fix his wounded heart or give him the role modeling he needed, that once he settled into his new apartment, he should find a good church to attend and seek out a godly man to mentor him.

"We'll probably never know if he followed my advice, but at least I tried. Because of what he did to you, I couldn't help him anymore; I needed to keep you as far away from him as possible. But I have been praying for Jay over the last few months, trusting God to lead him to someone who can help him."

I was completely caught off guard by this part of my dad's confession. Feeling a little hurt, I asked,

"Why didn't you tell me about this? Didn't you think I'd want to know? All you said was that Jay left the hospital once he knew I was all right."

"Keeping that conversation a secret was my way of protecting you again, honey. I didn't want you to go on feeling sorry for him and take the blame for what happened."

"I guess I can't be too mad," I sighed. "I never told you that Jay contacted me after I got out of the hospital. He left a note on the windshield of my car while I was in a café saying goodbye to some friends."

"What did the note say?"

"Just what he said to you—that he never meant to hurt me and to please forgive him. After I read the note, I ripped it up and threw it in the trash."

"Why didn't you tell me about it until now?"

"Maybe because I am like my father. We both seem to have a habit of keeping the wrong things secret to help the ones we love. As much as we hate to admit it, maybe our real motive is more about protecting ourselves."

"You're right. But even if our motives had been unselfish, I think we can both see that holding back the truth when it needs to be told doesn't end up helping anyone. After talking to John, I can see that my attempts to protect you from the unpleasant things in life only failed to prepare you for them.

"When you went away to college, you left the safety of home and were thrown into a totally different world. You had no idea there were men out there like Jay. That's why you believed everything he told you, letting him manipulate you into doing what he wanted. John felt like he'd let you down and asked for your forgiveness. Now it's my turn. Will you please forgive me for failing you, Julia?"

"Only if you'll forgive me, too," I said with a smile.

"Of course," my dad said as he got up from the table and gave me a hug. "But we still have a problem, don't we? What are we going to do about this habit we have of hiding the truth?"

"I don't know. What do you think we should do?"

"Let's not just say we're sorry. Let's sincerely repent. That means admitting we have a problem and choosing to change. Shall we make a pact?"

"Sure, Dad."

"Okay, let's pray and ask the Lord to help us. *Dear Father, Julia and I admit our weakness to You. We no longer want to conceal things for selfish reasons. We ask you to give us the courage to be honest with one another. In Jesus' name, we will do our best to be open and transparent, with no more secrets!*"

I added an amen to my dad's prayer as I gave him another big hug. "Now that that's settled, how about you two helping me get these dishes into the dishwasher," my mom said with a grin.

"Okay, but first, can you pray with me one more time? Cassie said I might still have an emotional tie to Jay. I'd like you and Dad to pray and break its hold on me."

"That's a good idea, sweetheart," my mom replied.

All three of us held hands as my dad prayed, *"Heavenly Father, we stand in the authority Christ*

*purchased for us as believers. In the name of Jesus, we
exercise that authority to break any emotional tie that
may still be between Julia and Jay and declare them
both free from this moment on. Thank you, Father, for
hearing our prayer."*

After praying, my dad laughingly asked, "Now are
you ready to tackle those dishes?"

"Yes, but first I need to do something." I picked
up the pictures and note from the dining room table,
tore them into pieces, and tossed them on top of a
stack of dirty dishes. "I can't tell you how glad I am to
get rid of these," I sighed in relief.

I could tell my dad felt relieved, too, now that I
finally knew the truth. At last, we could be a transparent family—one that could share everything—the
bad as well as the good.

Common Sense

The last few weeks of summer were spent filling out job applications and going on interviews. Finding a place to work that could accommodate my college schedule was harder than I'd anticipated. I was relieved to finally get a call from the director at Sunny Acres Rehabilitation Center. One of her aides had just quit, and she needed an immediate replacement.

I drove out to the Center that afternoon, and after interviewing with the director in her office, she offered me the job. I was happy to take it, even though my pay wasn't going to be all that great. At least my hours would fit in with my classes, and I might eventually get to work in their physical therapy unit.

I started there early the next morning, not knowing quite what to expect. As I walked the halls, learning my duties and getting to know the residents and the rest of the staff, I realized I wasn't prepared for the sights, sounds, and smells all around me.

Some people were there recuperating from an injury or illness, while the rest of the residents now called the Center their home. Many were confined to wheelchairs and simply sat in the hallways most of the day, waiting for someone to come by and help them. Others stayed in their rooms or in the front lounge, watching TV for hours or just staring out the window. Some still had their mental faculties; others did not. Those were the saddest cases because they'd lost not only their health, but also their memories and sense of identity.

At first, I found it hard to work there. The residents would constantly tell me how lonely they felt, how long it had been since anyone visited. I found myself fighting back tears when someone would beg me, "Please take me back home. Don't leave me here!"

I kept my composure at work, but there were a few nights in my room I broke down and cried. One night I poured out my heart to the Lord in my journal:

Dear Father,

I need Your help at my job. There's so much I want to do for the residents there, but I can't. There's no way I can stop them from growing older or fix their bodies, and I feel so helpless. I grew up in a fairy tale, not understanding real life and the pain it sometimes brings. Now that I'm seeing it up close, my heart feels like it's breaking. These people have lost so much and need so much. I really want to do more. What can I do, Lord?

I stopped writing for a moment and listened for God to speak to my spirit. I only heard four words: *Show them My love.*

Suddenly, I realized that while growing old and dying were unavoidable parts of life, I could show Christ's love to the people at the Center, helping to make those years in their lives the best possible. I started to see my time there differently, as more than just working a shift. I had a mission now, and that made me feel really good about going to work every day.

My second week on the job, I met someone everyone at the Center called Miss Lottie. She was an elegant and well-spoken woman in her early seventies who lived in the apartments next door and came to visit the residents every afternoon. She was a Christian, too, and we quickly became friends. It was refreshing to see someone so genuinely love the residents, and I learned a lot those first few weeks just spending time with her.

In fact, through Miss Lottie, I got to know each resident in my wing as a person with a unique life-story. Some of the stories were so interesting, I began writing them down, maybe to use in a book one day.

One of my favorites was about how Sophia Demarco had met her husband. Miss Lottie knew most of the details, so she was able to help Sophia tell me her story, filling in some of the parts that the ninety-year-old woman had trouble remembering.

Sophia had been born in Italy, and when she was seventeen, a friend of her father's living in the U.S.

wrote home, looking for a wife for his nephew. When she heard about the offer, Sophia quickly agreed to the arranged marriage. She had always wanted to live in America, and this was her chance.

It was at this point of the conversation that I asked, "How could you agree to marry someone you'd never met? Weren't you scared? You didn't even know what he looked like, did you?"

Sophia smiled before answering in her charming Italian accent, "Of course, I was a little scared to go. But I had a feeling it would turn out well for me. My family in Italy was poor, and so were my marriage prospects. I didn't want to get married just to be married. I wanted to better myself for the sake of my children. I knew America would give them opportunities that my small village never could. Besides, I was told I could come home if I didn't like the man, so I had nothing to lose.

"His looks didn't matter all that much to me as long as he had a kind and gentle nature. My father wasn't very handsome, but my mother was a beautiful woman, and she loved him very much. He was a good husband and father and remained faithful to her. She told me, 'Find a hardworking man who treats you well, and you will have a happy life. If he's not so handsome—good! Other women will leave him alone.'

"You girls today don't understand what a real marriage is," Sophia continued, shaking her finger at me. "You think it's like in the movies. Only movies are made-up stories about people. They're not about how life really is."

Laughing, I replied, "Maybe, Miss Sophia, but I still don't see how you could sleep with a man who was a total stranger to you!"

"Well, we didn't get married as soon as I arrived. I lived with his uncle's family for a couple of months before the wedding. I got to know Dino during that time and liked him. We got along and worked well together, so I chose to love him when I married him, and my feelings for him grew with time. We were very happy and had six children together, four sons and two daughters."

It was hard to believe people used to get married like that, but there were several residents on my wing with similar stories. One woman named Anna had made the trip from Europe to America to *escape* an arranged marriage!

I was glad that times were different now, that my dad wasn't making wedding plans for me regardless of my feelings. I could see how people could make an arranged marriage work, but I wanted to meet my husband without the help of a matchmaker. Maybe being single for now wasn't so bad after all!

Before I knew it, summer break was over, and it was time for me to start classes again. It didn't take long to get used to my new routine at Weston U. I was worried I wouldn't like it there as much as Tyler, but to my surprise, I liked it even better. The class sizes were smaller, and I enjoyed getting to know my professors. I was still taking required courses, but most of them were interesting.

It was fun living near Cassie again, and we spent most of our time on the weekends working, studying, and hanging out with the other singles from Weston Christian Center. Life became a never-ending merry-go-round of school, work, and church.

The Center director adjusted my hours to blend with my college schedule, forcing me to work two nights a week. I really didn't mind since the residents went to bed early and I could study at my desk between rounds.

Sometimes I would catch myself daydreaming on those evenings, thinking about the lives of the people I was taking care of on my wing. In a way, I could relate to Sophia's story. I felt like I was making a voyage into the great unknown myself, only I wasn't crossing an ocean to find my Mr. Right. I was staying in my hometown, trusting God to bring us together. But how long would I have to wait to meet him?

There was someone in my science lab I really liked. He was a Christian and part of our singles' group at church. Good-looking and fun, he always made me laugh when we were together. Could he be *the one*? Common sense would say *no*; I had years of school ahead of me. Still, my heart was secretly hoping...

Sister Talk

For weeks, I had been looking forward to winter break as a well-deserved breather. But instead of enjoying my vacation, I spent every day of it dealing with a broken heart. Things had not gone as I'd hoped with the guy in my science lab.

Those weeks sitting at home had given me too much time to analyze and mope. It actually felt good to be going to classes again. I was counting on the busyness of the new semester to make me forget all about him.

But deep down, I knew it wasn't going to be that easy. Even though Keith was no longer in any of my classes, he would still be at our church's Wednesday Bible study. And tonight was the first meeting since winter break.

"I really don't feel like going, Lord," I prayed as I finished getting ready. *"If he shows up, I might not*

be able to hide my feelings. But I know I'm a coward if I stay home. Besides, it's impossible to avoid seeing him again. By not going, I'm just postponing the inevitable. Please, Father, give me the grace to get through tonight."

Sighing, I went to my closet to pick out an outfit. After a few minutes, I decided on a denim skirt and the long-sleeved shirt I'd picked up at the mall the day before. "Maybe wearing something new will lift my spirits," I mumbled under my breath. Once my make up and hair were done, I went downstairs and said goodbye to my parents.

Pulling away from the house a few minutes later, I checked the clock in the car console. I was definitely going to be late. Actually, that was a good thing; now I could slip into the back of the room unnoticed.

But it didn't work out that way. The moment Cassie saw me walk in, she motioned for me to come sit up front with her. Scanning the crowd on my way to where she was standing, I didn't see Keith anywhere. Feeling more at ease, I greeted Cassie and some other friends sitting close by. The way the place was packed out, I was glad Cassie had saved me a spot. The only empty chair in the room was right next to mine, with a Bible lying on the seat to reserve it.

Everyone got quiet when the singles' pastor went to the podium and asked the group to be seated for the opening prayer. As he prayed, I heard someone slip quietly into the chair next to mine. When the prayer ended, I looked over to find Keith smiling at me.

Leaning over, he whispered, "Hey, I wondered where you were tonight; you usually get here early. You're looking pretty, as usual. Nice shirt!"

Instantly, my heart sunk in my chest, and I felt my face flush. Although I smiled and nodded, I really felt like smacking Keith for that flowery compliment. *It doesn't mean a thing*! I angrily thought. *They're just empty words.*

The pastor was already speaking by now, so I didn't have to talk to Keith. Throughout the message, I sat wondering if anyone else noticed how uncomfortable I was. Actually, nobody in the room—not even Cassie—knew what I was feeling. Only God understood what was going on inside of me.

I hadn't confided in Cassie about Keith because I admired her for keeping her feelings about Brian to herself for years—for refusing to dwell on those feelings or share them with others—for putting what Brian wanted and needed above herself—for totally trusting God with their relationship. I wanted to follow her example and keep from confessing things now that I might regret later, to be more unselfish and trust God completely. Only gaining that kind of maturity wasn't easy.

When the pastor finished preaching, refreshments were served in the back of the room. Unfortunately, this was even more awkward than simply sitting next to Keith—mainly because my rival, who had breezed in halfway through the meeting, was now hanging all over Keith, talking, laughing, and flitting around, happy as could be. It was all upsetting to me, so I strategically kept my distance. Being a pretty good actress, I managed to behave normally, keeping up the pretense that nothing was wrong.

But when I was finally back home, safe in my room, I broke down and cried, reliving all the emotion of what had happened almost a month ago. Only I didn't want to think about it anymore; I wanted to let it all go. But I couldn't for some reason, and I didn't understand why. Frustrated, I reached for my journal and wrote:

> *This is ridiculous, Lord. Keith and I weren't even dating. He isn't obligated to me in any way, so why can't I just be happy for him and go on without feeling so hurt, so betrayed? I think I need to talk to someone about this...*

Instantly, Jenny's name popped into my head, and I tacked on:

> *Should I talk to Jenny, Lord? I feel like I should...*

Seeing it was too late to call Jenny in Chile, I went to my laptop and sent her an email, asking her to meet online at eight o'clock the next night—Weston time. Then I typed, *"Please try to make it. It's important!"*

I was so anxious to talk to Jenny, the next day felt like it was moving in slow motion. My morning classes seemed longer than usual, and my afternoon shift at the Center dragged until I was finally off duty at five-thirty. My mom noticed I was a little edgy at dinner and asked if anything was wrong.

"No," I assured her. "I'm just anxious to get online and talk with Jen tonight. I have something I need to ask her."

"Well, give her and John our love. And tell her that tomorrow I'll ship those things she asked me for."

"Sure, Mom."

It was almost seven-thirty when we finished eating, so after helping Kitty with the dishes, I immediately went upstairs. At eight o'clock sharp I was online, waiting for Jenny to meet me. Just then, my cell phone rang.

"Not now," I groaned, annoyed by the bad timing. Grabbing my phone, I checked the caller ID. I was surprised to see it was Jenny.

"Jen?"

"Hi, Julia."

"Hey, I expected to meet you online tonight."

"I know, but it worked out for me to call you instead."

"That's great! I'd rather talk to you on the phone anyway."

"Is everything all right back home?"

"Sure. Why?"

"You said you wanted to talk about something important..."

"It is important, but just to me. I need to talk to you about something personal, that's all."

"What a relief! I've been a little worried since I got your message."

"Sorry if I scared you."

"That's okay. So, what's going on?"

"It's funny, Jenny. I've been so anxious to talk to you, but now that I've got you on the phone, I feel a little silly telling you about this."

"Why? If something's bothering you, you should tell someone. There's nothing silly about that."

"Maybe silly isn't the right word. Embarrassed is more like it."

"You don't have to be embarrassed with me, Julia. Come on, tell me what's wrong."

"Remember when I told you about a great guy in one of my classes last semester?"

"You mean Keith?"

"That's the one."

"And..."

"Well, I found out he was a new Christian, so I invited him to my singles' group, and he's been going to our church ever since."

"That's great! Is he what's been bothering you? Did you two start dating or something?"

"No, but I would've gone out with him if he'd asked. When we first met, Keith seemed really attracted to me. He was giving off all the right signals, and I was doing my best to let him know I felt the same way. Between class and church, we were together a lot, and it looked like we might start dating. This went on for several weeks. I never wrote any more about Keith because there wasn't anything to tell, really. So far, we were just being friends, even though I had a major crush on him."

"So what finally happened?"

"Right before winter break, a girl came up to me at one of our singles' meetings and told me how excited she was that someone had asked her out. I was shocked when she said the guy was Keith.

"Immediately, a flood of emotions surged through me: disappointment, jealousy, and the big one—rejection. I told Heather I was happy for her, but in my heart, I was anything but happy. I was furious. It felt so unfair since I'd been the one to introduce the two of them.

"Thankfully, I kept myself from falling apart until I got home that night. When I was alone in my room, I knelt by my bed and just sobbed. Then I asked the Lord why this had happened, why Keith would show such an interest in me and then go ask another girl out. Did I do or say something wrong? Was she prettier than I was? Did she have a better personality? What happened?"

"Did He give you an answer, Julia?"

"Not yet; I'm still waiting. When I asked Him about it again last night, your name flashed through my mind. I felt like I needed to talk to you."

"I think I know why."

"Why?"

"Because something like that happened to me, and I know exactly what you're feeling right now. Maybe hearing my story will help."

"Then tell me, Jen; I'm miserable."

"Okay, just relax for now and listen; this will take awhile. I met Craig my first semester at college. At that time I was still dealing with my mom's death, and I was also missing the closeness I'd always had with my dad. You know, the way he'd been before my mom died. Even though I understood that he was working through a lot of pain and wasn't himself, there were moments when it felt like I'd lost both my parents in that accident. Maybe that was why I fell so hard for Craig. I was lonely and wanted to feel loved again.

"Looking back, mine was pretty much the same situation as yours, only Craig wasn't a new believer. He'd been raised in a Christian home, but had gotten away from his faith during high school. Through an outreach at college, he'd rededicated his life to the Lord as a sophomore. I met him two years later on campus at a Christian meeting welcoming the incoming freshmen. We ended up sitting next to each other.

"I remember thinking how nice it was for all those upperclassmen to come meet the new students. That just shows how

naïve I was at that age. It never entered my mind that some of the guys were there just to check out the new crop of freshman girls.

"Anyway, Craig was really nice to me at that meeting, and when it was over, he took me around and introduced me to some of his friends. I definitely read into his attention, taking it as a sign that he was interested in me.

"We saw each other a lot after that meeting, on campus and at our Bible study group. It was always the same: he was charming and attentive, and I ate it all up, wondering when he was going to finally ask me out on a date. Then I heard Craig was interested in another girl from our study group, that they were going out that Friday night. I couldn't believe it.

"You see, Kristy was a single mom. She'd made some mistakes after high school and had gotten pregnant at college her second year. Now she was back home living with her parents, raising her son, and finishing her degree. She was a Christian and had been coming to our study group for quite a while. Actually, Kristy was a great person, and I liked her a lot.

"When I first found out Craig wanted to date her, I told myself nothing would come of their relationship. I was wrong. Craig

and Kristy got engaged not long after their first date.

"When you said you had to deal with a lot of emotions, Julia, I could relate. I had all those feelings, too, as well as some unanswered questions. Initially, I wondered why Craig would be interested in Kristy, knowing that marrying her would mean raising her son. I couldn't figure out why he would prefer her to me. In my mind, I was definitely the better, less-complicated choice.

"Sounds pretty self-centered, doesn't it? But that's where I was in that stage of my life, immature and self-centered. Because I was hurting, I was looking for someone to make me feel better about myself. My interest in Craig really came from a selfish motivation, but I was blind to it at the time.

"For some months after that, I had to fight rejection every time I saw them together. Eventually, I got tired of feeling sorry for myself, and while I was praying one day, the Lord showed me some things I hadn't considered.

"First and foremost, Craig had never been God's choice for me. He'd been my choice for me. I wasn't even ready for a permanent relationship because of my stage of life and where I was in the grieving *process with my mother. I still needed time to mature and heal.*

"Secondly, I wasn't a better choice for Craig just because I hadn't had a child already. Kristy had put her sin under the blood of Jesus; she'd sincerely repented and had believed God for a new and better life. The Lord saw her from that point on as someone who had never made a mistake. He viewed her as one of His special daughters, entitled to have a wonderful husband and a devoted father for her son. It wasn't chance. God was the One who brought Craig and Kristy together because He knew they were both ready for a love that was willing to follow after Him and sacrifice for one another.

"Those feelings of rejection left when I finally realized something: when someone pushes you away or fails to notice you, you don't have to take it personally. What feels like rejection today can actually be God's protection over you and your future. He alone knows which relationships will be best for you during the different stages of your life. I had to learn to trust Him to develop the right relationships and remove the ones that weren't intended for me.

"Now I thank the Lord for protecting me when I was so vulnerable and could've settled for the wrong man. Even though

Craig was a good Christian man, he wasn't my Mr. Right. He was Kristy's Mr. Right. I learned through my experience with Craig to do a better job of guarding my heart— not to jump to conclusions—to test every relationship with time and prayer.

"God was saving me for John and him for me. I'm so glad I didn't run ahead of the Lord and insist on doing things my own way. If I'd gotten more involved with Craig or with some other man, I might've missed out on meeting John. It scares me to think how easily that could've happened. I thank God every day for the privilege of being John's wife. He was worth every minute I had to wait for him, and I can honestly say I love him more today than the day we were married. Is any of this helping, Julia?"

"So much, Jen. Now I know why God wanted me to talk to you. I need to release Keith and Heather into God's hands and pray He makes their relationship into whatever He wants."

"Good for you."

"You know, Jen, when I was in high school, I went through an awkward time when I didn't feel very pretty."

"Most girls feel like that at some time, Julia. I'm sure we all have school pictures we're hiding somewhere, ashamed to admit we ever looked like that."

"Probably, but did you know I was over-weight when I was in fifth and sixth grade?"

"No, I didn't."

"Well, I was, and other kids teased me about it, two boys especially. They made fun of me a lot, and I started to feel bad about myself. When I told my mom, she helped me to see that most of what they said wasn't true at all. I had picked up some extra pounds, but that was because I wasn't getting much exercise and had been eating too much junk food with my best friend. She could eat anything she wanted and not gain an ounce, but it was starting to show on me."

"You mean Cassie?"

"Yes. She still eats like a horse and gets away with it. Anyway, I realized I had a different metabolism than Cass, and I started eating better. That summer John began taking me to the Y with him, and he taught me to play racquetball. By the time school started in the fall, I'd lost those extra pounds, and Mom bought me some new clothes.

"Even though I'd lost the weight I needed to, the poor self-image I had in my mind wasn't that easy to erase. When I went back to school, I was sure the boys would notice how much better I looked and say something nice for once. They didn't. That same year I got braces, and later on, I had to deal with major pimples. Ugh! Talk about some bad school pictures—I've got them!

"My dad wouldn't let me date in high school, so Jay was really the first guy, besides my dad and brother, who made me feel beautiful. That's probably why I fell into his trap so easily. Then, when Keith chose Heather over me, those old feelings of rejection came back again."

"You think that's why you've had such a hard time dealing with the Keith situation?"

"Definitely. But after our talk tonight, I know I don't have to feel rejected anymore. There's nothing wrong with me just because Keith or any other guy isn't interested in me romantically. I can relax, knowing God's constantly on the job, always protecting, keeping my heart in reserve for my future husband, just the way He did for you and John. I think as soon as I pray and release Keith, the pain of not dating him will start to go away."

"I'm really proud of you, Julia."

"Thanks, Jen. I'm glad we had this sister talk. Oh, I almost forgot—Mom said to give you and John her love and to tell you that tomorrow she's mailing the things you asked her to send."

"Tell her thanks, and give her and Dad a hug for me."

"I will."

"Have you told Mom anything about Keith?"

"Not much. She knew I had a crush on him for a while, but that's all."

"Why don't you tell her about our talk? I'll bet anything she's had a Keith in her past, too. Maybe even some school pictures she's kept out of sight."

"I think I will. Maybe at breakfast tomorrow. Dad has an early appointment, so we'll be alone. Thanks again for calling tonight, Jen. Talking on the phone was so much better than meeting online."

"It was a lot less work, too! Can you imagine typing out everything we've said?"

"No way! Give my brother a kiss for me."

"I will."

"I miss you guys so much!"

"We miss all of you, too. But your brother is doing something really important here in this community. You should see how much it's changed already. I'm convinced I married a genius."

"John proved that when he married you."

"Oh, I so love having you for a sister!"

"Ditto. And you're doing just as much as John is there, you know. From what he tells us, the clinic really needs you."

"I do love working here, and I've been volunteering when I can at an orphanage not too far from our home. The kids are all

***so precious, Julia, so hungry for love and
attention."***

"See, God has you there for a reason, too."

***"Thanks, I agree. Well, it's been great
talking to you, but I'd better go for now."***

"Me, too, Jen. Goodbye."

"Bye."

That night, I prayed and finally released my feelings for Keith to the Lord. The next morning, I had a great talk with my mom. Jen was right. She had a romantic rejection in her past, too. She also showed me two school pictures she kept under the lining in her jewelry box. They were pretty awful.

When I asked her why she'd kept them, my mom replied, "Every now and then I take them out and look at them. They remind me that with God, all things improve with time."

I was learning to appreciate that truth more each day. Once I dealt with my feelings for Keith in a mature way, I found I was able to be around him and Heather and be truly happy for them. The pain didn't go away immediately, but it did go away eventually. Although I'd taken a small detour, I was now back on track, going about my busy life, waiting to meet my true love, unaware that another rejection problem was just around the corner.

Chapter 8

Unwanted Admirer

Classes and my job at the Center were continuing to go well. Spring break had already come and gone, and soon I'd be gearing up for final exams. Fortunately, work, school, and church were keeping me so busy there was little time for romantic fantasies. Even so, I prayed for my future husband whenever I could and often wrote little notes to him in my journal, intending to read them to him once we were engaged. Just the night before I had written:

> *Mr. Right,*
> *What are you doing now? Are you thinking about me, too? Asking yourself who I am or what I'm doing? I pray God helps you to sense that I'm keeping myself just for you, waiting for you to come and find me. I can't help wondering if you're far away or very close by. Maybe I'm passing you every day on campus without even knowing it!*

There was a time when waiting for you just made me sad, but now I appreciate this time of separation. I understand God is working on both of us so we can be more of a blessing to each other when we're finally together. I'm trying to cooperate with God as He develops what's needed in me for you. I'm hoping you're cooperating with Him, too.

Then, I added a prayer: *Lord, from my talk with John, I know my man is fighting some strong physical desires. Please protect him from the seductress described in the Book of Proverbs, and help him to keep himself just for me. In Jesus' name, amen.*

Although I was dateless, I had to admit that things were going great in my life, with one exception: I had recently picked up an unwanted admirer. About two months earlier, a visitor had shown up at one of the singles' meetings. I had already met him my first semester at Weston while paying my tuition. He was none other than Alvin Avery, a.k.a. Flip the Mechanic.

Flip became a regular with the singles' group after that first night and started going to all the church services as well. Before long, it was obvious to everyone that he had a big crush on me.

One of the other singles led Flip to the Lord shortly after he joined the group, and knowing he was still a baby Christian, I didn't want to do anything to discourage him from coming to church and growing in his faith. So, even though I wasn't interested in him as a boyfriend and wished he'd stop bothering me, I kept my lips sealed and simply tried to downplay his attention.

Unfortunately, the more I ignored him, the more he pestered me. He constantly embarrassed me in front of other people by calling me *the most beautiful girl in the world.* If that wasn't humiliating enough, he would even ask someone right in front of me, "Don't you think Julia's the greatest—the smartest—the prettiest?" What did he expect them to say with me standing right there? Although I never said anything when he did those things, the rolling of my eyes as I turned and walked away would've given any other guy the message I was *not* happy.

While my friends at church thought all this was funny, they knew I didn't like Flip as more than a friend, and that consoled me. At school, however, it was a different story. Flip had been pointing me out on campus and telling other students I was his girl-friend. I was getting tired of explaining to people I barely knew that Flip was definitely *not* my boyfriend.

Once finals were over, I went into the summer breathing a sigh of relief, confident that Flip's extended hours at the garage would keep him too busy and too tired to chase after me. No such luck! Apparently, all Flip thought about while working on cars were ways to drive me crazy.

He started calling me at night when he got home from work. "Hey Julia," he'd start out. "Bet you were thinkin' about me, huh?" No matter how many times I answered with a loud *no*, he never got the point. I now understood the meaning of *selective hearing.*

If he hadn't been such a new Christian and so committed to the singles' group, I would've told him to back off long ago. Not knowing what else to do, I just tried to be patient until his infatuation with me went away. Meanwhile, Flip found out my schedule at the Center, and one night as I was leaving through the lobby, he popped up from a wing-backed chair near the front door.

"Hey, Julia girl. Is that a *buy-me-a-pizza* look in your eyes? I think it is," he said with a smirk, fully expecting me to jump at the chance to go out with him.

It was almost eleven. I couldn't believe he was even asking this late. "No thanks. I'm tired, and I just want to go home."

"Cool! I'll drive you," he instantly offered.

"I have my own car, Flip," I responded, irritated.

"So, I'll follow you home. Beautiful girls like you shouldn't be drivin' at night alone. Some nutty guy might see you and try to bug you."

I bit my tongue to keep from blurting out, "Some nutty guy *is* bugging me!"

Refusing to hear an objection, he walked me to my car and followed me home. Pulling into the driveway, I drove straight into the attached garage, immediately closing the door behind me. Flip had no other choice than to drive off without so much as a goodbye.

"Forgive me, Lord," I prayed as I walked into the house and up to my room. *"I know that wasn't very nice, but I don't know how else to make Flip understand*

I don't want to be his girlfriend. Nothing I do seems to work, and I don't know what else to try."

I sputtered and complained about Flip the whole time I was undressing and getting ready for bed. It wasn't until I was under the covers and almost asleep that I was quiet enough to hear God say, "Just tell him you don't want to be his girlfriend."

"Is that You, Lord?" I whispered under my breath as I turned over and settled into a more comfortable position. *"That sounds almost too simple to work."*

The next morning was Saturday and, incidentally, my day off. My parents had an early appointment at the office, and Kitty was scheduled to clean the house. Looking forward to sleeping in, I'd hung on my doorknob the *Do Not Disturb* sign that Kitty had made for me years before. Whenever she saw it, she knew I wanted to keep sleeping and waited to clean my room last.

Everything was going according to plan until a few minutes before eight. Ignoring the sign on my door, Kitty poked her head inside my room and softly asked me for the keys to my car.

"What...?" I mumbled as I sat up, still half asleep. "Why do you need my keys?"

"Sorry I woke you," Kitty apologized, "but the man at the door needs them to take your car in to be serviced."

"My car? Serviced?" I questioned, rubbing my eyes, confused. "There's nothing wrong with my car." Then it dawned on me. "Oh, no. Flip's here!"

Informing Kitty I'd be down in a minute, I angrily flipped off my covers and headed to the closet. I couldn't remember being this angry with anyone for quite some time. "I don't know what that pest is up to now, but I'm definitely going to find out!" I raved, slipping into some sweats.

After pulling my hair back into a ponytail, I scooped up my keys off the dresser and stormed out of the room, all set to wave the keys in Flip's face and demand an explanation for showing up at my house so early, uninvited. Fortunately, by the time I got downstairs, I had calmed down enough to be civil when I met him at the door.

I barely had a chance to say *hello* before Flip started running off at the mouth. "I knew it! You even look beautiful in the a.m. with no makeup and your hair kinda pushed back. Not many girls can do that, ya know what I mean?"

Infuriated, I began to retort, only to be cut off again. "Bet you didn't expect to see me first thing today, huh?" he chuckled, grinning as he rocked back and forth on his heels. "Anyway, I'm here 'cause your car's not runnin' right, Julia. I noticed a knockin' sound when you started it up last night. I got time to work on it this morning, so I come by early to get it and take it down to the garage with me. And don't worry—it won't cost ya nothin'," he assured me, patting me on the shoulder, trying to eliminate any objections I might have to his plan.

Giving me no chance to respond, he kept going. "I can fix that knockin' easy, Julia, no problem. Can't have you ridin' in a car that's not safe, ya know? Tell ya what, I'll bring it back after I get off work and pick up my truck then. What'dya think?" he asked, already assuming my answer would be *yes*. "And hey, no thanks necessary, beautiful. Glad to do it. Gotta take care of my girl, right?"

I just stood there in disbelief, my mouth wide open. Too frustrated to reply, I simply handed him my keys and shut the door in his face. He would've been shocked to know I had no intention of thanking him. The only word running through my mind at the moment was *strangulation!*

Since I was now wide-awake, I decided to stay downstairs and have some breakfast. When I finished eating, I called Cassie to fill her in on these last two encounters with Flip.

"When Flip comes back with your car tonight, tell him you don't want to be his girlfriend," she suggested.

"That's what I felt the Lord told me to do," I admitted.

"So do it! I still don't get why you haven't done it already."

"I probably should have, Cass, but I kept hoping it wouldn't come to that. I don't want to hurt his feelings."

"I'm not sure you have a choice anymore, Julia. He's not getting the message by you just ignoring him. The only way to end this is to tell him the truth in love."

"Okay, I'll talk to him about it tonight when he brings back my car. Pray for me. You know how much I hate confrontation."

"I will. You can tell me at church tomorrow how he took it."

Saying goodbye, I hung up the phone, ran upstairs, and got in the shower. As I rinsed the conditioner out of my hair, I suddenly realized I didn't have a car now. So much for my plan to run errands that day. "Thanks a lot, Flip," I complained out loud, turning off the water.

Once I'd finished in the bathroom, I walked back to my room and slipped into some comfortable jeans and a T-shirt. As I combed through my damp hair, I looked over at my desk computer and spied the email message I had opened the previous day from one of my friends from Tyler U. Karen and I emailed each other a lot since saying goodbye at school almost a year ago, and she kept me updated on what was happening in the lives of our mutual friends.

Occasionally, I'd get a text message from Gary or Kenny saying *hello*, but they weren't into sharing too many details. My former sorority sister, Gretchen, was better about keeping in touch. After becoming a Christian, she'd quit the sorority and roomed with Karen in the dorm her last year at Tyler. Gretchen and I emailed each other often.

My day wide open now, I sat down at my desk and re-read Karen's email. After several lines, a smile broke out on my face as I thought about what a good friend she'd been to me at Tyler. I missed spending time with her.

"I'm disappointed your old roommate hasn't answered any of my emails," Karen had written. "I know you've tried to contact Fran, too, and Gretchen said she has texted her lots of times but got no response. I guess we'll never know what she decided to do about her *unsolvable problem*, as she always put it. I wish I didn't feel so bad about losing touch with her."

I felt the same way, maybe even more so. After all, if Fran hadn't called Gretchen when she did, I might not be alive today. My friends and I wanted to be there for Fran during her time of crisis, but she had slammed the door shut on all our efforts to help her.

I typed a reply to Karen, trying to console her. I ended with: "We've prayed and believed the best for Fran and her situation, and now she's completely in the Lord's hands. It's time for all three of us to stop worrying once and for all. God will take care of her."

Sighing, I hit *send* and leaned back in my chair. Spinning around, I surveyed my room, trying to figure out what to do with my day now that I was stuck at home without a car. I decided to just relax, replying to more of my emails and reorganizing my closet.

My parents already knew what was going on with Flip, and they were glad to hear at dinner that I was going to talk to him that night. "I haven't wanted to interfere, honey," my dad said, "but if he bothers you any more after tonight, I'll have to step in and set him straight."

"I hope you won't have to, Dad. I want to handle this myself."

I had my chance a few hours later when Flip returned my car. He said he changed the air filter and gave the car a good tune up; that's all it really needed. This time I did thank him. Then I invited him to come talk with me for a minute out on the back patio.

After pouring us both a soda in the kitchen, I led Flip outside to the patio table, where we both sat down. He was grinning from ear to ear, obviously misunderstanding my reason for asking him to stay.

While Flip was taking a big gulp of his drink, and before he could start his usual string of comments, I nicely explained that while I liked him as a friend, I was not interested in him as a boyfriend. I braced myself for his reaction, but his expression stayed the same, almost as if he hadn't heard what I'd said. He simply sat there and smiled at me like a Cheshire cat. Finally, I asked him, "Did you hear what I said?"

"Sure. Ya said ya didn't want to be my girlfriend."

Actually, I had said I wasn't interested in him as a boyfriend, but since he got the general idea, I didn't bother to correct him. I just nodded, totally unprepared for what he said next.

"That's just 'cause ya don't know me good enough yet. Trust me, Julia; I'll grow on ya. Ya just gotta spend more time with me. I'm a patient guy, ya know what I mean? Just give us a chance. How about goin' to the movies with me Saturday?"

"No, Flip! You do understand *no*, don't you?"

"Sure I do. But *no* tonight could be *yes* later," he responded in his goofy manner. "Like I said, I'm real patient."

At that moment, I couldn't relate; I'd already exhausted my patience with him. Exasperated, I exclaimed, "I'll *never* say yes to a date with you!"

"Ya know what they say," he sang out smugly. "Never say never!"

"All right, I think you'd better leave. This isn't getting us anywhere!"

"Okay! Okay!" he said, leaning back in his chair, holding up his hands. "I can tell you're gettin' mad at me." Taking a deep breath, he reached over and touched my hand. "But I love ya, Julia. Ya just gotta love me back. If ya don't, I don't know what I'll do. I might go outta my mind I love ya so much. Hey, I might even kill myself!"

I refused to be taken in by that. "That choice is up to you, Flip, but you're not going to get me to date you by threatening to hurt yourself. I can't love you just because you like me."

"But ya *will* love me, Julia. Ya don't know it now, but someday you're gonna marry me. Just wait and see."

"That does it!" I shouted, getting to my feet. "I'm so fed up with this! When I was at Tyler, there was a guy who chased after me and insisted I was going to marry him, too. His selfish love almost killed me!"

"Oh, yeah?" Flip broke in. "Who is this jerk? I'll take care of him for ya!"

"Gee, thanks," I snapped back sarcastically. "Flip, the only jerk I need you to take care of for me is *you!* Actually, that other guy could teach you a lesson. At least he finally realized you can't force someone to love you. You obviously don't get that yet!"

"Maybe you're right, Julia," he conceded, his head down. "I just thought that lovin' ya as much as I do, you'd just have to love me back."

Feeling sorry for Flip and a little ashamed of myself for losing my temper, I dropped to my chair again and tried to explain in a more reasonable tone of voice. "Listen, Flip. There are different kinds of love people feel for each other. The love I feel for you is a friendship love, not the romantic kind of love. I can't make myself feel something that isn't there. Someday the right girl will come along, and she'll be able to return your love."

"Ya think so?" he asked, looking up.

"Sure I do. God has the right someone planned for each of us. All we have to do is trust Him to bring us together with them at the right time."

"And you're real sure I'm not the right person for ya, huh?"

"Yes, I'm sure."

"Ya still mad at me, Julia?" he asked apologetically.

"Not anymore. Not as long as you understand I'm your sister in Christ and *not* your girlfriend."

"If that's the way ya want it," he said reluctantly. "I guess I'd rather lose ya as a girlfriend than lose ya as a friend."

"I agree," I said with a smile. Thanking him again for fixing my car, I walked Flip off the patio, around the side of the house, and out to his truck where we said good night.

As he pulled away, I thanked God that the matter was finally settled. The only regret I had was in not confronting him sooner. If I'd told him how I felt when I first noticed his attraction to me, he wouldn't have spent so much time dreaming about something that was never going to happen.

"Please forgive me, Father," I prayed on my way up the front steps and into the house. *"I knew better than to let things go on this long. I guess I have a weakness for putting off until tomorrow what my heart knows I should be doing today. I'm trying to get better at that. Thanks for being patient with me, in Jesus' name."*

From the foyer, I could see the back of my dad's head as he sat reading in the living room. "How'd it go?" he asked, looking up from his book as I perched beside him on the armrest.

"Flip agreed we would just be friends from now on."

"Well done, Julia. I'm proud of you. It takes courage to tell people the truth when you know their feelings are going to be hurt. How'd he take it?"

"Before or after he said I was going to marry him someday?"

My dad shook his head and just chuckled.

"Tell me, Dad. What is there about me that makes men think they can decide *for* me that I'm going to marry them?"

"Some men like to lead, Julia; others like to push. So far, you've met a couple of real pushers. But don't lose heart. When the right guy comes along, he won't have to push; you'll want what he has to offer you."

"I can hardly wait," I answered longingly. Giving my dad a goodnight kiss, I went back out to the patio to clear off the table. Once I placed Flip's glass in the dishwasher, I refilled mine and headed up to my room to spend some time with God before bed.

Sitting at my desk, I read several Bible passages and then wrote a short prayer in my journal:

> *Thank you, Father, for giving me the courage to talk to Flip tonight. Help him to deal with any rejection he may be feeling—the same way You helped me with Keith. As it turned out, I'm glad I didn't get involved with him. When Keith stopped dating Heather right after graduation, it broke her heart. Apparently, all he had wanted was someone to have fun with until he graduated. If I'd been the one to date him, I would've been hurt like Heather when he moved back home. Thanks for protecting me.*
>
> *I realize that with so much school still ahead of me, it's probably a little early for me to meet my Mr. Right. But wherever he is tonight, please tell him I love him already.*
>
> *Mom was right; these long months of waiting will make me appreciate him more once we're finally together. It will be wonderful to finally put all dating issues behind me and just relax and concentrate on loving the one and only man in my life...*

The next day at church, it was obvious to all the singles that something had happened between Flip and me. His whole demeanor had changed, not only towards me, but towards everyone else as well. He was polite, but distant and acted a little put out. Cassie told me not to feel bad about it. Flip was just disappointed, and God and time would help to heal his wounds.

Cassie was right. By the time school started again in the fall, Flip was back to normal. Better, in fact. He had met with the singles' pastor a lot over the summer and switched his major to business management. He had hopes of owning his own auto repair center one day, and with a fresh outlook on his future, he'd come to accept that the two of us weren't meant to be more than friends.

While I was glad that everything with Flip had turned out so well, I couldn't help but still feel a little discouraged. So far, all my experiences with guys were failures. Dating Jay had been a disaster, Keith had never asked me out, and while Flip was crazy about me, I wasn't attracted to him at all.

"Father, when will I finally find the right guy, someone who likes me as much as I like him?" I prayed, starting to pout a little. *"Sorry,"* I added, catching myself complaining. *"It's just that I want this so much, it's hard to see the big picture. I love You, Lord. Thanks for always keeping Your promises to me, for preparing great things I can't even imagine right now.*

"I know You've got everything under control, Lord, but can I make a request? Until my Mr. Right gets here,

can You please send me a close guy friend to hang out with? I think that might make the wait a little easier. Well, it's an idea, anyway..."

Tall Paul

Hanging up the phone, I grabbed a piece of scrap paper and jotted down the appointment I had just made for that afternoon with my student advisor. Already into the second half of Christmas break, I was hoping it wasn't too late to switch one of my classes for the coming semester—my *fourth* at Weston U. How time was flying!

Meanwhile, emails and text messages were still keeping me current with what was happening to my friends from Tyler. Gretchen and Gary had graduated the previous year and were both involved in the youth program at their church. In fact, Gary had recently become the youth pastor there. Reading between the lines, I was pretty sure they had become more than friends. My suspicions were confirmed when Gretchen called one night to tell me they were dating.

Three months later, I received a card announcing their engagement.

Karen was in love, too. She had met her boyfriend several months earlier at a missionary conference and wrote me all about it, sending a picture of the two of them taken that first weekend. Although I was happy for my friends, I couldn't help feeling a little envious because of the void in my own life, romantically speaking.

My devotional time with God truly became my life source. It seemed that no matter how tired I was before bedtime, I couldn't rest until I'd read my Bible or shared my heart with God. Reaching for my journal on the corner of my desk, I opened it to the entry from the previous night:

> *Father, my life is so rich and full, I hardly know how to thank You. Somehow, mere words can't express the gratitude I feel in my heart for all the ways You've blessed me. Grandma Helen says it's good to thank You out loud, reciting our blessings. Since I've been doing that, I've experienced a deeper awareness of Your goodness.*
>
> *Please don't take this next part the wrong way. You're everything to me, and I love You with all my heart. But when the weekends come, I'm reminded that my Mr. Right isn't here yet. The compartment You made in my heart for him is empty and longs to be filled. I'm choosing to be happy for now, but it's not always easy.*

Please take care of him wherever he is. Keep him safe, and in Jesus' name, please make sure he finds the path that will lead him to me.

Closing the cover to my journal, I slid it to the corner of my desk and gave it a pat, as if to add an *amen* to what I'd just read. Sighing, I sat back and listened to how quiet it was with my parents away. They had been gone for three days now, and I was beginning to feel engulfed by the emptiness of the house.

Two weeks earlier, my parents had received an email from John and Jenny announcing their decision to adopt a little girl from the orphanage near their home in Chile. Jenny wrote: "The first time I sat Magda on my lap, I knew I was holding our daughter, that God was going to give her to us. She's seventeen-months old and absolutely adorable. John fell in love with her the minute he looked into those big brown eyes. What a little character she is! All giggles and smiles and hugs. We didn't want to get our hopes up and tell you about her until we were sure we could adopt her."

When my parents read the news, they immediately made plans to fly to Chile. While they were anxious to meet little Magda, they were just as excited to see John and Jenny again. It had been almost a year and a half since they had left for South America.

Since I was on winter break, I initially hoped to go as well. But in the end, I couldn't get enough time off from work. It was disappointing to have to stay home, but my dad promised to take lots of pictures and videos.

I had asked Cassie to stay with me while my parents were gone, but her grandmother had just undergone eye surgery and needed help in Tipton for a few days. Cassie was there with her. I would've hung out at my grandparents' place, but they had just come home from visiting my uncle's family, and I felt they needed a few days alone to rest up from their trip. Kitty was out of town, too, vacationing at her daughter's, so I was on my own.

When my afternoon appointment with my counselor was over, I decided to drop by the mall close to campus. I didn't really need anything, but I was feeling a little down being by myself on a Friday night. Maybe a little shopping would help.

I wandered around the mall for a while, stopping into a few of my favorite stores, not seeing much that interested me. Finally, I passed by a store with a huge winter clearance sign in the window. Sorting through the sale racks there, I carried an armful of outfits into the dressing room.

I liked almost everything I tried on, but trying to be sensible, I put a few things back before taking the rest to the checkout counter. As I stood paying for the clothes, my stomach started growling, attracting both the clerk's and my attention. Blushing a little, I looked down at my watch.

No wonder I'm hungry! I thought, seeing it was past seven already. Returning my checkbook to my purse, I slipped the strap up onto my shoulder, grabbed up my bags, and headed straight for the food court in the center of the mall.

Making my way to my favorite vendor, I scanned the choices on the menu board and opted for a slice of deep-dish pizza. Once a salad and drink were added to my tray, I paid the cashier and looked down at my meal, wondering how in the world I was going to get it to a table while carrying all of my bags at the same time.

"Need some help?"

I turned to see one of the guys from our singles' group standing beside me, amused by my dilemma. "Hi, Paul. Would you mind?"

"Not at all. Where do you want to sit?"

"Over there's fine," I decided, pointing to a nearby spot.

"Okay, let's grab it while we can," Paul suggested, taking my tray and leading the way through the crowd to the empty table.

When he set my food down, I asked, "Would you like to join me? Are you hungry? Or would you just like something to drink?"

"Yes and no and no," he answered with a smile as we both sat down. "Julia, do you realize you rapid-fire questions at people?"

"I know; it's a bad habit. Sorry."

"It's okay," he assured me as he removed the paper from my straw. "Go ahead and pray. I'll just sit while you eat."

I bowed my head and asked a silent blessing on the food. When I was done, Paul pushed the straw

into the lid of my cup and started our conversation with a mild rebuke. "So, how come you never told me what a good racquetball player you are? I watched you beat Jeremy and Adam at the outreach last Wednesday. I couldn't believe how good you were."

"Why?" I asked, pretending to be offended.

Squirming in his seat, Paul fumbled for an answer. "Ah...I don't know why. I was just surprised, that's all."

"But why were you so surprised?" I persisted. I had him backed into a corner, and he knew it.

"I just didn't think a girl could power the ball that hard."

I laughed and answered, "Truthfully, I don't think Adam was playing all out against me. As for Jeremy, he hasn't played that much."

"Maybe, but you are really good. How'd you learn to play so well?"

"My brother taught me. I love playing with him."

"My game's basketball," Paul replied.

"Yes, I know. Cassie told me you were a basketball star in high school."

"Thanks, but I wouldn't say I was a star. We did have a great team though, and we won state my senior year."

"Why aren't you playing at Weston?"

"Blew out my knee in a pick-up game right before college. It still bothers me when I play too much."

"That's too bad, Paul. I'm sure you're disappointed."

"Yeah, but there's nothing I can do about it. I guess I have more time to study this way."

"You're majoring in accounting, right?"

"Right. You're P.T., aren't you?"

"Yes, I'm just starting my fifth semester."

"That's great. The next time my knee gives out, I'll know where to go for therapy."

"You'd only be an experiment for me right now. Better wait until I've earned my degree," I advised him.

"Maybe you're right," Paul replied with a grin. "I'll try to hold off getting injured until you do." Casually looking down, he checked his watch. "Hey, I was going to see *Ryan's Crossing* tonight. It starts in an hour at Cinema 12. Want to go?"

"Depends. What's it rated?"

"Don't worry; Pastor Mark saw it and said it was great."

"All right, that's good enough for me."

We talked a few minutes more while I finished my food. Then Paul returned my tray while I put on my coat and scooped up my bags and purse. "Should I meet you at the theater?" I asked when he rejoined me.

"Good idea. Where are you parked?"

"Ah...the south entrance, over by Skyler's."

"I'm out that way, too. Let me help you carry this stuff to your car, and you can drive me to mine. Then you can just follow me."

"Okay," I agreed, passing off three of my bags to Paul.

The two of us talked and laughed as we made our way to the car. I had been quite melancholy when I arrived at the mall a few hours earlier, but now I felt carefree and lighthearted—grateful for somewhere to go and the chance to get to know *Tall Paul*, as the rest of the girls in the singles' group affectionately called him.

The movie was a complicated mystery, and I continually whispered questions to Paul to keep up with the plot. He didn't seem to mind, even though he was missing some of the show when he stopped to explain something. Nothing about the story was predictable, and we both enjoyed it, especially the ending.

By the time I got back home, it was past midnight. After hanging up my coat in the mudroom, I stopped in the kitchen to make some tea to take upstairs. While the tea was steeping, I checked the voicemail messages on our home phone. The first was from my student advisor, confirming the changes we had agreed upon in her office earlier that day.

The next one was from Cassie, and it sounded urgent. "Julia, I tried to get you on your cell phone around eleven, but I couldn't get through. It must've been turned off. I'm hoping you get this message at the house before you go to bed. I've got some-thing—maybe the flu—and I can barely take care of my grandma. Could you drive down here in the morning and give me a hand? Don't call me tonight; I'm going to try to get some sleep. Phone me first thing tomorrow."

Cassie's voice sounded awful, and I was worried she was really sick. I reached for my mug of tea and marched directly upstairs to throw a few things into a bag so I could shower, dress, and leave at first light. Because it was so late, I decided to do my devotions in bed instead of at my desk. After my nightly rituals, I slid between the sheets, propped up some pillows behind me, and opened my Bible to read.

Look at me, I thought as I read. *I look just like my mom, minus the glasses, of course.*

I was thinking about how my mom always read her Bible at night in bed. Many times she would fall asleep, and my dad would take the Bible and set it on the nightstand with her glasses, which he had carefully removed from her face. Then he'd turn out the light and go to sleep as well.

My mom told me she often woke up when my dad did all that, but she purposely remained quiet, as though she were still asleep. "Those are special moments for me, Julia," she confessed, "because your dad's gentleness makes me feel so loved by him."

My reminiscing made me miss my parents even more while they were away. Picking up my journal and a pen, I wrote:

Heavenly Father,
I want a man like my dad. I want a marriage like my parents and grandparents have. Please don't let me get impatient and settle for anything less. Your Word assures me that if I keep trusting, I'll eventually receive what You've promised. I need Your grace during my wait for the promise to be fulfilled.

Even though I know You'll be faithful to give me the husband of my dreams, there are still times when my mind is overwhelmed with the fear that it will never happen for me, that I'll always be alone.

Will I be meeting him any time soon? I know I still have four more years of school ahead of me, but...

After writing a few more paragraphs, I closed my journal and turned out the light, needing to get some rest before my three-hour drive to Tipton. Unfortunately, I wasn't the least bit sleepy. I just kept tossing and turning, trying to get comfortable.

Once I finally got settled, I started to think about how bad Cassie had sounded on the voicemail. If she hadn't identified herself, I wouldn't have known it was her. The more I thought about how sick she sounded, the more my concerns grew. Then the *what ifs* started. What if her grandmother needed something in the middle of the night and Cassie was too weak to help her? What if this? What if that? I couldn't help envisioning the worst.

After lying in bed for over an hour, worried senseless, I finally decided to throw on some clothes and get on the road. That way, I'd be there even earlier to help Cassie.

Daffy Dinah

Twenty minutes after my decision to start for Tipton, I was pulling out of the garage. I was glad I had filled my tank with gas the day before. It might be hard to find a filling station in some of the remote little towns I'd be traveling through, especially at this hour. Pausing for a minute in the driveway, I reached for the plastic case I kept under the front seat and pulled out a few of my favorite CDs. Traveling always went faster with some good music.

A little over an hour later, I was making great time on the country roads Cassie had shown me the previous summer. After traveling for a while without seeing so much as a billboard, I finally spied one of those no-name filling stations with a little store attached. Thankful it was still open at 3 a.m., I pulled in to get something to drink.

Once inside, I picked out a soda and went to the counter to pay for it. As I turned to leave, I noticed a weird-looking man hanging around up front. The way he was eyeing me up and down made my skin crawl. Refusing to look at him, I quickly hurried to my car and got back on the road again.

Driving along, I was having trouble shaking the creepy feeling from the store a few miles back. I couldn't help but think that if my dad knew I was making a trip this late at night by myself, he'd be pretty upset with me. I had to admit this wasn't one of my better ideas.

I had more than enough gas to get to where I was going, but that wouldn't help if I blew out a tire or had some kind of car trouble. I would be totally unprotected if I got stranded along the road somewhere. My cell phone was in my purse, but who would I call in unfamiliar surroundings like these? Too bad I hadn't thought this all through before leaving in the middle of the night.

"Dear Lord, my intentions were good. All I wanted to do was help a friend. In Jesus' name, please forgive me for taking a foolish chance. Protect me, get me there safely, and let me..."

My prayer was cut short by a tap on my back bumper. Startled, I looked in my rearview mirror and saw another car right on my tail. I slowed down a little, thinking the driver wanted to pass me, but the car hit my bumper even harder the second time. Quickly checking my mirror again, I tried to see who was driving behind me. But I couldn't. It was too dark.

Terror struck me. Was this the man from the store? I felt sure that it was. "Jesus, help me!" I immediately cried out, my heart pounding. Frantically scanning the area, I realized there were no other cars in sight. I grabbed my cell phone out of my purse and dialed 911. It rang twice and then cut out. The words *low battery* were flashing.

Bang! The third and hardest blow to my bumper sent the phone flying out of my hand as the car lunged forward and swerved toward the middle of the two-lane highway. I sensed my attacker was through toying with me, that his next move would be to force me off the road. Clutching the steering wheel with both hands, I prayed to God for help to outdrive him.

My intuitions were right. The other driver was now trying to pass me, first on the left, then on the right. But no matter how he tried to gain the advantage, I was able to position myself to block him. It was as if God Himself were guiding my hands as they worked the steering wheel.

Fortunately, on this straight stretch of highway I was able to stay just enough ahead of the other car to keep it from bumping into me from behind again. The intensity of this contest was mounting with every second, and I remained white-knuckled at the wheel. I couldn't think about how long I'd have to keep this up before finding some outlet for help.

I thought about honking the horn, but there were very few houses on this road anyway, and I needed both hands on the wheel. Out of the corner of my eye, I saw a sign that warned of a sharp curve ahead.

"Dear God, help me!" I shrieked in desperation, still swerving to avoid being passed.

All at once, my headlights lit up a bridge ahead. The bump at the entrance lifted my car into the air, and it landed a few seconds later with a loud thud. The sharp curve awaited me just as I crossed the bridge, and accelerating too fast, I lost control in the turn, my tires slipping off the pavement and into a steep ditch beside the road. Slamming on my brakes, I held on tight as the car skidded down the embankment and crashed sideways into the trees below.

Locked inside my vehicle, I laid on the horn in a desperate attempt to attract someone's attention—anyone who might be near enough to help me. I began crying so hard I could barely see, panicked by the fear that at any second, my attacker would be outside the car, trying to break in.

Suddenly, I noticed a flashing red light in my rearview mirror and backed off the horn. The next sound I heard was a rap on my window. I screamed and ducked my head.

"It's all right, Miss! I'm with the police!" a man called to me.

I turned to the side window and saw a beautiful sight—the officer had his badge pressed against the glass so I could clearly see it. Still badly shaken, I fumbled around trying to find the lock release. When I pressed it, he opened the door.

"Are you hurt, Miss?"

"I...I don't think so," I answered, my voice quivering.

"Let's get you out of the car and see if you can stand up," the officer suggested.

I obediently swung my legs out, reached for the officer's hand, and let him pull me to my feet. But the adrenaline rush was over, and drained of all strength, my knees buckled at first. The officer caught me and braced me up until I regained my balance. When he felt I was steadier, he said, "You won't be driving this anywhere tonight. Do you think you can walk up to the road and get into my squad car?"

I weakly nodded I could, and the officer helped me make my way up to his vehicle, placing me in the back seat. After calling in to the dispatcher, he turned to me and asked where I kept my registration.

"It's in the glove compartment," I replied, still trying to catch my breath from the trek up the hill.

"I need to get it. You stay here while I'm gone; I'll lock you in for safekeeping. You've had enough excitement for one night," he said with a smile, trying to put me more at ease. At my request, he also brought back my keys, purse, and overnight bag.

"Did anyone catch the man who was chasing me?" I asked when he returned with my things.

"No, Miss. At least I didn't. He turned off onto one of these back roads when he saw me coming. I didn't chase after him because I was afraid you might be hurt. I called in a description of his car and the direction he was headed, but I think he got away." Noticing I was still trembling, he asked me again, "Are you sure you're not hurt?"

"I'm okay, really," I assured him, rubbing my neck where the seatbelt had restrained me during the crash. "I'm sore here and there and still feel a little shaky, that's all. Thank God you were in the area to help me, Officer...?"

"Bremen. But you can thank your friends for tipping me off, or I wouldn't have been anywhere near here. Your name is Julia, isn't it?"

"Yes, how did you know?" I asked, taken aback.

"I stopped at a filling station in Dawson, and two guys in bowling shirts walked up to me and said a young woman named Julia had just been there—that a man was watching her the whole time she was inside the store. They said they heard him mumble something about *catching up with that girl* before he got into a late model gray coupe.

"So I went after him. When I eventually caught up, I could see his car in the distance swerving from side to side, trying to run you off the road. You'd better be glad those guys told me about him following you. What are you doing out here this time of night, anyway?"

"Actually, sir, I'm on my way to help a sick friend. When I left home, I never expected anything like this to happen."

"It happens all the time, Julia. Take my word for it. Like I said before, if your friends hadn't been around, that guy could've raped or even killed you."

The reality of what might have happened hit me, and I started to cry. Embarrassed, I quickly composed myself and admitted, "You're right, and I'm grateful to be alive. I have to tell you, though, I have no idea who told you about me. Nobody around here knows me. Did you get the names of the men?"

"Sort of. I was in a hurry to get out of there, so I just read the names on their shirts. Damon and Daryl sent me your way. Do you know them?"

My jaw immediately dropped. "Just someone named Daryl. He helped me out once before when I was in trouble." The officer didn't respond, momentarily absorbed in copying down the information from my registration.

"So, there are two of them..." I mused quietly to myself.

"Two of what?" the officer asked, overhearing my remark.

I looked over at him a bit sheepishly and grinned. "My guardian angels. I have *two* of them!"

The officer smiled back and nodded in an attempt to humor me, choosing not to comment on that last statement, certain I was still in shock. He merely said, "I'm going to take you to the police station in Bradleyville. When we get there, I'll finish my report, and you can call someone to come pick you up."

I was just starting to recover from the trauma of my ordeal, and now I had another situation to face—calling my grandfather. I really had no other choice since Cassie was too sick to come get me and my parents were on another continent.

As soon as we arrived at the police station, I made the call. I briefly explained what had happened, and

my grandpa assured me that he and my grandmother would leave as soon as they got dressed.

Waiting for them to arrive seemed like the longest two hours of my life. The moment my grandparents walked through the police station doors, I ran to hug them. With my head on my grandpa's shoulder, another flood of tears spilled out.

Once I had calmed down, the three of us found a hallway bench where we could sit as I gave a detailed account of all that had happened. They comforted me as best they could and were ready to take me back home. But I was determined to go to Tipton to be there for Cassie.

I pointed out, "Regardless of what happened, Cass still needs my help. The police called a towing service to bring my car in for repairs. I don't know how badly it's damaged yet, but I can call the repair shop and insurance company later today. Cassie is planning on coming back to Weston on Monday, so I'll ride back here with her and pick up my car if it's ready by then. If it's not, Cass can bring me the rest of the way home."

Since I wasn't hurt, my grandparents agreed to take me to Tipton. While we were driving, my grandma decided to use my unfortunate experience as a teachable moment. She asked me if I knew the story in Genesis 34 about a girl named Dinah. When I shook my head *no*, she went on to tell me what had happened to that girl.

"Jacob and Leah had a daughter named Dinah. When she was just a young woman, Dinah decided to leave her home and visit some other young women who lived in that area, *unattended*, the Amplified Bible says. At some point a young man, a prince in fact, noticed her beauty, lusted after her, and eventually found a way to sexually violate her. The story goes on to record the many people who were killed as a result of that attack on her.

"Now, the prince was completely wrong for what he did to that young girl. Whether he forced her or seduced her, it was inexcusable. This situation was very serious, and at the end of the story, the prince paid for that crime with his life! But there's something else I want you to understand, Julia. Had Dinah made some different choices herself, she might have been spared such a traumatic experience.

"Young women haven't changed all that much throughout the years, sweetheart. They may talk and dress a little differently, but inside they're just the same. They like male attention, and they can often act very silly and make unwise choices to get it.

"Sometimes a girl will try to gain a man's attention through the way she looks at him or by wearing revealing clothing. It's all a harmless game to her, but since men can be sexually motivated, female indiscretions can become an overwhelming temptation.

"The Bible doesn't say how that prince was able to get Dinah into a compromising situation. You have to read between the lines. We're simply told that he 'saw her.' Well, where did he see her? Was she traveling by herself? Was she going to places or parties that gave her the wrong kind of exposure? Was she continually flirting with him and, therefore, sending him the message, '*I might be willing*?'

"The Bible goes on to tell us that '...he took her and lay with her, and violated her.' How was he able to do that? Where was she when he took her? Was she alone and in unprotected surroundings? Was she initially willing to go with him or did he force her from the start?

"Scripture doesn't reveal exactly what happened. Dinah may have been making mostly good choices and simply found herself in the wrong place at the wrong time. Or she may have gone off with the prince alone, thinking they would just get a little physical—you know, maybe do some kissing. After all, it would be flattering to be pursued by a powerful prince!

"We won't know the entire story until heaven, but we can learn from it all the same. Once a girl recognizes how vulnerable she is, she should be mindful of the situations she puts herself in. Someone else might be to blame for a horrible experience, but that doesn't change the pain she has to work through afterwards. She still has to cope with what's happened, whether or not it was her fault. That's why God wants us to take responsibility for ourselves as His daughters and make the best decisions we can concerning our safety.

"As women, we're often targeted for abuse. We tend to be trusting by nature, and if we aren't careful, we can be deceived, seduced, or overpowered by a man. When women sneak around or secretly do things, they have to rely solely on their own abilities to protect themselves. Taking off for Tipton late last night by yourself, Julia, was like putting a big bull's-eye on your forehead. You became fair game for violent men like the one you saw in that gas station."

My grandpa broke in. "Three of the things God uses to help keep you safe are: wise choices, the truth, and the light. The enemy of your soul will always try to get you to make bad or rash choices, believe lies, and enter unprotected places. That's why you need to consult with godly people before you do things.

"When you decided to go help your friend, your heart was in the right place, but you weren't thinking clearly. In my opinion, women have no business traveling alone late at night. Few businesses are open at that hour, and there's little traffic on the roads. Most sensible people are at home in bed.

"I want you to think about something, Julia. If you'd been hurt, raped, or killed last night, your whole family would've been forced to live through that nightmare. From now on, try to remember that your decisions affect not only you, but everyone who loves you. Please don't be a daffy Dinah anymore."

I promised my grandparents that I'd never make such a foolish mistake again. When we pulled into Cassie's grandma's driveway, I checked my watch. We were arriving an hour *later* than I would have had I left early in the morning the way Cassie suggested. So my hasty decision hadn't worked to my advantage at all. Instead, it had cost me a good night's sleep and even endangered my life.

When Cassie opened the front door for us, it was obvious she was still very ill, so we only gave her a brief recap of what had happened. Knowing both Cassie and I could use some rest, my grandparents took over running the house while we slept. When they left for home after supper, the house was clean, Cassie's grandmother was already in bed for the night, and a big pot of homemade soup was sitting in the refrigerator.

Life looked much brighter the next morning. I was well rested, and although Cassie was still feeling a little weak, she was much better. It wasn't until after breakfast that we had a chance to talk in detail about the frightening chase the night before.

When I finished my story, Cassie asked, "Do you think it was the same Daryl who helped you with Jay? You know, the guy your mom thought was an angel?"

"You tell me, Cass. What are the odds that two strangers would know my name and that one of them would be named Daryl? I didn't see any men in bowling shirts when I was in the store that night. The only other person in there besides me and that creepy-looking man was the woman behind the counter."

"There doesn't seem to be any other explanation, Julia. They must've been your guardian angels. I've heard that every Christian has two angels assigned to them for life. Know what I think?"

"What?" I asked, leaning forward in anticipation.

"I think if I were Damon and Daryl, I'd ask to be reassigned. You're getting to be too much trouble, even for angels!"

"Very funny," I groaned, rolling my eyes.

Cassie laughed. "I've never understood how you could keep such a high GPA and still make so many dumb mistakes!"

"You're going to see a big difference in your best friend from now on, Cass. Something inside of me changed last night. I got scared into being much more mature."

Current Events

Monday morning, I called the body shop in Bradleyville to check on my car. The mechanic informed me that the right side had been substantially damaged, but not enough to total the vehicle. He also said there was no way it would be ready that afternoon. In fact, he wouldn't even be ordering the necessary parts until completing his assessment later that week.

"Mistakes are easily made but not easily remedied," I murmured as I slowly hung up the phone. Although I was disappointed, I had to count my blessings: I hadn't been hurt in the crash, except for some bruises and sore muscles, my car was covered by insurance, and my parents' cars were at home for me to use.

Although everything was working out okay, I wasn't looking forward to telling my mom and dad about my latest mess up. I knew they would be glad I was safe, and they rarely got angry about fixing or replacing anything. Still, I dreaded having to face them and admit to making more choices that put me in harm's way.

I kiddingly wondered if my parents would ever leave me by myself again. As much as I wanted to be treated like a responsible adult, it was obvious I didn't always wisely use the freedom they gave me.

Later that morning, Cassie and I left for home as planned. On our drive back to Weston, we stopped at the curve by the bridge to see where my car had gone into the ditch. The skid marks on the pavement and the ruts left by the tow truck were tangible proof of the recent attack and rescue I'd experienced.

As we continued driving, Cassie could tell I was reliving some of the stress from that night. Trying to lighten the mood, she jokingly offered to stop for a snack at that same filling station in Dawson.

"No thanks," I replied with a shudder. "That place is off limits for me. I'm not in the mood to meet any more weirdos!" That got us laughing, and I was back to myself for the rest of the trip. By the time we reached Weston, we had agreed to stay together at my house until my parents got back from Chile.

"Actually, it's not safe to leave you alone too long," Cassie teased as she pulled into my driveway. "I'm sticking close to you from now on."

"That's one of the drawbacks to making stupid mistakes," I grumbled as I removed my overnight bag from the car. "Although God forgives and forgets, some people love to keep reminding you."

Cassie just grinned. Then, as she was backing out into the street, she lowered her window and called out, "That's because some people only learn through repetition!"

The grandfather clock in our foyer struck six as I walked into the house. Shutting the front door with my hip, I set my things down and went straight to the phone to call Flip. When I explained to him what had happened, he blew up.

"What kinda car did you say that jerk was drivin'? An old model gray coupe? That's a good lead, Julia, 'cause it's probably gettin' serviced somewhere close by. I'll put the word out to all the repair shops around Dawson. All I want is five minutes alone with that guy!"

"Calm down, Flip. The police think the car was stolen."

"Yeah, right. Who goes around stealin' cars like that?"

"The officer said that men who run girls off the road usually don't want to bang up their own cars and use stolen ones instead. He's sure the car from Friday night will turn up on a country road someplace."

"So you're tellin' me that loser's still out there, waitin' to strike again, and there's nothin' the police can do about it?"

"Not until they catch him in the act, Flip."

"What were you thinkin' anyway, drivin' by yourself that late? You should've called me. I'd have taken you, and none of this would've happened."

"That's the trouble, Flip; I wasn't thinking. I was just reacting to Cassie's message when I decided to leave in the middle of the night like that. In a way though, you *did* help me. You got my car running so well, I was able to keep ahead of that guy for most of the chase."

"Where's your car now?" Flip asked.

"It's at a body shop in Bradleyville."

"They start workin' on it yet?"

"No, they said they wouldn't even order the parts until later this week."

"Good. If it's okay, I'll take the tow truck down there tomorrow, pick up your car, an' work on it myself. Our body man's real good, too. When I finish my part, he can do the rest."

"Thanks, Flip. I was hoping you'd offer. If *you* fix it, I know it'll be done right."

"Not a problem, Julia. I still like doin' things for ya."

As soon as I was done talking to Flip, I called my grandparents to let them know I'd arrived home safely and to give them an update on my car. Then I threw a load of clothes in the washer. Knowing Cassie would be back in a couple of hours, I checked the pantry to see if I needed to make a trip to the store. Fortunately, my mom had stocked the house with more than enough groceries.

For the next seven days, Cassie and I had a great time together, enjoying every minute of our remaining vacation from school. Cassie had access to my closet and loved wearing my clothes all week.

Between our work schedules, we cooked, baked, shopped, and rented some favorite movies. We talked and laughed until our sides ached. We were what best friends should be. We loved and accepted each other, even though we were different in so many ways. Our friendship was something special, and we both knew it.

By the time my parents returned from Chile, Cassie had moved back home and second semester classes had already begun. I spent my parents' first night at home recapping the last couple of weeks. My dad stared at me in disbelief as I told the part about my accident. Once I finished, he shook his head and said, "When I finally give you away at your wedding, I'm going to celebrate! Then I'll start praying for my son-in-law; he'll need all the help he can get."

My mom didn't say a word. She just patted my dad on the shoulder and rolled her eyes the way she always did when she was adding her agreement. I was glad my parents didn't scold me. They were just grateful I was all right, and with the danger past, they figured I'd already learned my lesson.

The rest of the evening was spent looking at pictures and watching videos of their trip. Magda was adorable, and John and Jenny were already devoted to her. Although the adoption wasn't official yet, it was just a matter of time and paperwork before everything would be finalized.

The following days were pretty normal around our house. My parents were back at work, Kitty finally returned from visiting her daughter, Flip had my car fixed good as new, and I was either working or studying.

I was especially enjoying my evening Ethics class. Professor McNulty was a good lecturer and always had interesting stories and insights to share. Because I had some free time before my night shift at the Center, I would occasionally sit and discuss different subjects with him for a while after class. He seemed to welcome and enjoy our talks all semester as much as I did.

As final exams approached, I began staying up later than usual, studying. With all the hours I was putting in at school and at the Center, I was exhausted—more than ready for the term to be over.

When I arrived at my last Ethics class for the semester, I was glad I wasn't scheduled to work afterwards. I was looking forward to going straight home after the session and getting some sleep.

Everything was going according to plan until class was dismissed. As I was leaving, Professor McNulty called to me, asking me to stay for a moment. The last thing I wanted to do was get into a lengthy conversation with him, but I couldn't ignore his request. Feeling obligated, I turned around, walked back into the classroom, and waited by his desk. There were already several students congregating around him with last-minute questions about the exam on Friday. By the time the professor was able to speak to me, everyone else had left.

"I'd like to discuss something with you, Julia, but I've had about all of this classroom I can take for one night. Let's get out of here and enjoy some ice cream while we talk," he suggested. The malt shop on campus was only a short walk from the building, so I reluctantly agreed. I figured I could grab a quick cone and be on my way home in no time.

Gathering up his things, Professor McNulty ushered me into the hall, and together we walked down the stairs. Suddenly, the professor took an unexpected turn, leading me out the side door of the building.

"I've got my car right here," he said, pointing to his black sedan parked close to the building. "Hop in."

I looked at him a little surprised since I had pictured us walking down to the malt shop. Unsure of what to do, I went around to the passenger side of his car and awkwardly got in. As he pulled away, I felt incredibly uncomfortable. What would other students think if they saw me riding with him? Students often talked with their professors on the school grounds, both in classes and at the campus cafés, but a girl riding around with a male professor in his car sent out a completely different message.

Oh, great! I thought as I slouched down in the front seat, intentionally placing my hand by my face to keep anyone from recognizing me. *How in the world did I get in this predicament?*

My concerns accelerated when we breezed right past the malt shop and headed off campus. "Where are we going, Professor McNulty? I thought we were getting a cone at Wally's."

He looked at me and smiled. "I know a much nicer place, Julia—without all the background noise."

The two of us made small talk as the professor drove, but my thoughts weren't focused on our conversation. I was thinking, *Here I am again, in a compromising situation, because of my inability to read men correctly. Now what am I going to do? Maybe the whole thing is innocent, and all he really wants is to talk to me about something. I'm probably worrying for nothing. Still, why the long drive off campus? Father, I hope Daryl and Damon are watching all this. I may need them again. Please help me, in Jesus' name.*

Eventually, we pulled off the highway and drove up to a small restaurant on the outskirts of town. Parking the car, the professor turned to me and said, "This place has the best ice cream around. Or maybe you're hungry and would like something more to eat?"

"Ice cream's fine, Professor McNulty," I quickly answered, feeling a little safer now that we were at a public place.

"Classes are nearly over, Julia. Let's drop the formalities. Just call me Don."

I'd rather not, I thought to myself. I didn't wait for him to come around and open my door. Instead, I quickly jumped out of the car and started for the entrance to the restaurant.

"Hey there! You're with me, remember?" the professor called out, trying to be funny, finally catching up to me at the door.

Once we were seated inside, he ordered my ice cream and a martini for himself. As soon as our order arrived, I asked him point-blank what he wanted to talk about.

"Us."

"Us?" I repeated, questioningly.

"Yes, Julia. I think we've become good friends during the last semester, and I enjoy our talks. Now that summer break is almost here, I'd like to get to know you better and start seeing you outside the classroom."

I was dumbfounded. I never dreamed that my occasional staying after class would give him the impression I was interested in him romantically. Now he was sitting across the table from me in a remote restaurant, waiting for my answer about dating him. The timing was really unfair, too. I had an essay final for his class on Friday. If I refused, I was sure my rejection of him would be reflected in my grade.

Thinking fast, I said, "I'd really rather we didn't think about that until after all my finals are over. Between school and work, I'm already close to burnout. We can talk more about it sometime next week, if you don't mind."

"All right, Julia. I'm going out of town for a week or so after finals. I'll call you when I get back."

"That'll be fine, Professor McNulty."

"Don, remember?"

"Oh, sorry," I mumbled, still skillfully avoiding the use of his first name.

Temporarily appeased, the professor was willing enough to call it a night when I explained how over-tired I was. As soon as I finished my dessert, he insisted upon paying the check, and we got back into his car. Wanting to score points with me, he drove directly back to campus, and we said a quick good night.

On my drive home, I found myself thanking God over and over. He had helped me think on my feet and get out of a tight situation, and I just couldn't stop praising Him. I chided myself for being so naïve, but at least I was maturing. Instead of trying to handle the professor myself, I went to my parents for help as soon as I got home. They were both in bed, reading, when I passed by their room.

"Can I come in for a minute?" I asked, peeking around the door.

My dad put his book down. "Sure, sweetheart. We're awake." He and my mom both turned their attention to me.

I walked over and sat down beside my mom on the bed. "Well, it looks like I've done it again. I'm in the middle of another big mess."

Knowing my past record, my parents braced themselves for what was coming. For the next few minutes, I explained to them about my professor—about our frequent talks after class and the way he had misinterpreted my friendliness. My mom and dad both praised me for the way I had handled myself with him. They also agreed that putting McNulty off

until my grade was finalized was a smart move on my part.

"I don't mean to lecture you, honey," my dad began, "but you need to know that when an attractive girl pays special attention to a man—any man, married or single—she's in danger of sending him a message he interprets as, '*I want more.*'

"I do a lot of legal work for the university, and I've talked with Don McNulty a few times. He isn't one of the school's full-time professors. He's a businessman in town who just teaches a few night classes. He's also a bachelor with a big ego and a reputation with the ladies. That man must be close to fifty years old. What he's suggesting to you is way out of line in my book. The sooner you put a stop to all this, the better."

"What should I say if he calls me this summer?"

"Tell him the truth," my mom advised. "Say you aren't interested in seeing him socially. If he's any kind of a gentleman, he'll let it go at that and leave you alone."

"I hope you're right, Mom, but I'm too tired to think about it anymore." Kissing my parents good night, I went to my room, got ready for bed, and fell asleep after reading only a few Bible verses.

Studying for my Ethics final over the next two days was even more pressure-filled than it would've been normally. I dreaded seeing Professor McNulty again, even though the room would be filled with other students.

Friday eventually rolled around, and it was time to sit for my exam. The professor was busy talking to another girl when I arrived, allowing me to slip quietly into my seat. I had just started to feel a little more comfortable when I heard him call my name. "Miss Duncan, will you please assist me in handing out the exam papers?"

Feeling eyes on me from all around the room, I slowly got up from my desk and walked to where the professor was standing at the front of the class. Holding out a stack of papers to me, he made forced eye contact, smiling in a way that made me blush. When I reached out and took the exams from him, he made sure he touched my hand, sending a sensual charge through me that only I could detect.

Trying to act as normal as possible, I pushed down my feelings of repulsion and turned to distribute the papers. I was still a bit flushed when I returned to my seat and silently prayed as final instructions were given for the exam.

"Father, in Jesus' name, help me to get through this test—to focus on the questions and answer them correctly. Quiet my heart. Still my mind. This unfortunate experience will be behind me once I walk out of this classroom. Please forgive me for anything I may have done to contribute to this problem."

After my prayer, God seemed to help me quickly recall the material I'd studied, and I completed every question with ease. Because I was one of the first to finish, I was able to turn in my exam and leave the room without any further contact with the professor.

"Thank you, Lord! Thank you, Lord!" I inwardly chanted, sprinting down the stairs, eventually

making my way out the front door of the building. "Free at last!" I sighed.

As I reached the front walkway, I felt strange, as if someone's eyes were following me. Looking around, I saw nothing at first. But then, panning up to the second floor of the building where I had just finished my exam, I saw Professor McNulty sitting on the inside ledge of the open classroom window, watching my every move. When he saw that he'd caught my attention, he gestured as if to say, "Be seeing you."

On the drive home, I couldn't remember how I'd responded to the professor's wave. Did I wave back? Did I smile? Or did I act like I hadn't seen him? I was positive he knew I saw him. *"O Lord, I was so rattled at the time, I'm not sure what I did. What if he thinks I'm snubbing him? How's that going to affect my grade?"*

 No, that's wrong!" I reprimanded myself. "I can't think like that. No grade is worth all this anxiety. If he lowers it because I'm not interested in him, then so be it. I'll deal with it then. But I refuse to try to appease him any longer."

I finished up my last exam the following Wednesday. Done with studying for a while, I was excited to shove the books aside and soak up some sunshine on my days off from the Center. The director had scheduled me for straight days during the summer so I could get some experience in the physical therapy wing. That meant I'd be off evenings and weekends, which made me very happy—more time for some much-needed recreation.

Paul and I had been playing racquetball a few times a week since our meeting at the mall. So far, I had come close, but hadn't been able to beat him. After every close match, I would tease, "I could've won that one, but I didn't want to push you so hard you'd injure your knee again."

That always made Paul laugh. Yet it also took some of the edge off the victory for him. He was pretty sure I was just kidding, but knowing how well I played, he sometimes wondered if I were holding back. I had fun keeping him guessing.

After racquetball, we'd usually have dinner together at Benny's Place down the street. The singles' group met there a lot, and it had become everyone's favorite hangout. Cassie would often stop in after finishing her shift at the paper mill, and Brian made it a point to know her schedule and be there when she came in. It wasn't uncommon for all four of us to show up around the same time and sit together. Those times were the best—no romantic involvement, no expectations, just laughing and having a good time.

A couple of weeks into my summer break, the dreaded phone call came. Fortunately, no one was home, and the professor left a message on our voicemail. "Hi, Julia. It's Don McNulty. My business took a little longer than I expected, but I'm back in town again. Let's meet for lunch. Call me." Then he left his cell number.

When I came home from work that afternoon, my mom played the message for me. "What should I do?" I asked, anxiously.

"Your grades came in the mail today, honey, so you don't have to worry about that anymore. He can't reverse the A you earned. Call back and discretely tell him to get lost. If he won't take *no* for an answer, say your parents think he's too old for you, that we don't want him calling you anymore."

"Okay, here goes," I responded, tentatively entering his number. Slowly putting the receiver up to my ear, I hoped he wouldn't answer, that I would get his voicemail. Unfortunately, he picked up after only two rings.

"Hi, Professor McNulty. This is Julia."

"I thought we agreed it was Don from now on."

I didn't answer him. After several moments of silence, he asked, "So, which day is good for you to have lunch this week?"

"Actually, I need to be honest with you," I began. "I'm sorry if I gave you the impression I wanted to see you outside of school, but I don't. I enjoyed taking your class and the talks we had, but I'm not interested in dating you."

"Well, let's not call it dating, Julia. I'd just like to get to know you better. I like talking with you and getting your perspective on current events. What's the harm in that?"

"I don't want to do that," I reiterated, emphasizing my words in a way that any intelligent person would have understood.

"Just think about it," he persisted, ignoring my answer. "I'm sure once you get past seeing me as your professor, you'll change your mind. I'll call you again next week."

"Please don't. My parents said there's too much difference in our ages, and my dad doesn't want you calling me. Thanks for understanding," I added before quickly hanging up the phone, cutting off his chance to say anything else.

My mom walked over and gave me a big hug. I was trembling. "I'm proud of you, sweetheart. I know that wasn't easy. Why do we women often fight feelings of guilt and fear when we have to tell a man *no*—even when he's pushing us to do something we don't want to?"

"I don't know, Mom, but I do seem to attract pushers."

A wave of relief sweep over me after my call to McNulty. I probably couldn't avoid seeing him again, but I was hopeful I wouldn't have to face that possibility before returning to campus in the fall.

At dinner, my mom asked me to relay the phone conversation to my dad. He scoffed at McNulty's line about wanting to see me *to talk about current events*. "I don't know who that guy thinks he's fooling. The only current event he's interested in involves taking you to bed with him."

I didn't counter my dad's last statement because I agreed with him. No matter how cleverly Professor McNulty had tried to disguise his motives, I had gotten his message loud and clear when he touched me on the day of the exam. The sensation that ran up my arm had nothing to do with friendship; it had been unmistakably sexual.

Chapter 12

S.O.S. Online

It was the first Sunday in June, and classes had been over for weeks. I was just beginning to relax and enjoy some summer fun between my hours at work when our church youth pastor pulled me aside after the morning service. He was starting small groups with the teens and wanted to know if I'd lead one for the girls.

"I'd love to, Pastor Kevin," I replied, "but I'm surprised you're asking me, knowing how I messed up my first year at college."

"You're not the same person who made those mistakes, Julia. You have a much stronger relationship with God now, and I think you'll be a good role model for the girls. Use your experience to help them avoid the mistakes you made."

"Okay, I'll try. How many girls will be in my group?"

"No more than ten; I want to keep the groups small. Cassie, Danielle, and Lindsay have agreed to be leaders, too. Can you come to a meeting before church tonight at five? Sorry about the late notice."

"Sure, I'll be there."

"Good. We'll meet in the youth room," Pastor Kevin informed me as we exited the church together. "See you at five," he added over his shoulder, jogging toward his car to where his family was waiting.

Ten minutes later, I pulled into a parking spot at the restaurant where I was meeting Cassie for lunch. Her car wasn't there yet, so I went inside and got a table. I'd been seated for some time before Cassie finally came in and found me.

"Sorry I'm late," she apologized, sliding into her seat. "I had to run an errand for my mom." Just then, the waitress brought our meals. "Hey, thanks for ordering for me. How'd you know what I wanted?"

"I knew you'd be hungry, as usual, so I just ordered food. You do eat about anything when you're hungry, don't you?"

"Ha, ha! So funny," Cassie retorted, tucking a flyaway wisp of red hair behind her ear.

"Besides," I continued, "you always order the special here."

"Yeah, I guess I do. Know why?"

"No, enlighten me," I responded, rolling my eyes.

"Because the special always comes with dessert."

Laughing, I bowed my head, and Cassie prayed over our meal. As we sat eating, we discussed the small groups Pastor Kevin was starting. I pointed out that although the groups would help us get to know the teens better, a girl could act like a Christian at church while still making serious compromises in her private life.

Cassie agreed. "That's true, and there's no way to know who might be doing that. Sometimes it's the ones you least expect."

"Like me, for instance?"

"Yeah, like you, Julia. I've been your friend for years, and you kept your life at college a secret from me. You were the last person I'd expect to act that way."

"I know, Cass; I never expected it from myself."

"So, some of the girls in our groups may be doing the very same things, or at least are heading in that direction."

"Exactly. And as we teach them the Bible, we've got to help them open up and share what's going on in their lives."

"That won't be easy, Julia. Look what it took to finally get you to tell all."

"Good point. Some things are too personal to share with everybody, especially when you know you've made mistakes. No girl likes to admit her weaknesses or failures."

Cassie's eyes suddenly lit up. "Hey, what if there was a way to share a story with the group without the group knowing who shared it?"

"Huh? You lost me there. How could they do that?"

"They could do it online."

"Explanation, please; you know I'm not that computer savvy."

"We'll set up a web group on the Internet, and the girls can share anything they want under a code name. They can submit questions and concerns, and we leaders can answer them online."

"Okay, keep going..."

"Each group leader could set up a night during the week to meet online with her girls. And if a girl couldn't log on at that time, she could still post a message on the site that we could read and respond to later..."

Sitting there listening, I started to catch the vision for this web group. I smiled, thinking about what could be accomplished through such a non-threatening line of communication.

"You know, Cass, when I was living a double life at school, I could've used a program like this. I wasn't ready to admit to my parents or friends what I was doing. I was too ashamed and too proud. But I desperately needed to talk to someone."

"Maybe we can give these girls that chance, Julia. Once they see they're not alone, that other girls are experiencing the same pressures and temptations, they might be more willing to open up and talk."

"And they need to. Trying to handle problems on your own just invites trouble. Look what happened with me and Jay."

"You know, I think you need to talk to all the girls before we actually start our small groups. If Pastor

Kevin agrees to it, we could have a retreat at your grandparents' cottage."

"Okay. Maybe the other leaders will have something to say, too, and sharing our stories will help explain the need for the small groups."

"That's it!" Cassie shrieked.

"What's it?"

"The perfect name for the web group. We'll call it *S.O.S. Online—Sharing Our Stories Online*. What do you think?"

"It's perfect."

"Let's see what Pastor Kevin says at the meeting tonight."

"I need to take a nap before then," I replied, stifling a yawn. "Paul and I went out last night, and I got to bed late. If you're done eating, I'm ready to go."

Taking one last bite of her cherry pie, Cassie nodded that she was finished. As we were paying our checks at the counter, she poked me and asked, "Hey, what's going on with you and Paul? You two are hanging out more and more lately."

"I know, Cass, but really, he's just a good friend." Once we were outside the restaurant, I added, "Since we're being nosey, when are you going to give Brian the green light? I feel sorry for him."

"I'm not the one controlling that, remember? When the time's right, God will let Brian know."

Before getting into my car, I couldn't resist teasing, "Then you'd better get ready—I think it's going to be soon!"

Cassie just smiled and held up her crossed fingers. Once she was inside her car, she lowered the passenger-side window and asked me to pick her up around four-thirty.

At the meeting that night, Danielle and Lindsay loved the idea of the web group. Pastor Kevin initially had some concerns about the content of the messages shared online, whether things would be said that weren't appropriate. Cassie assured him she would act as the moderator and set things up so that nothing was viewed or sent out without being monitored. She promised that if anything was questionable, it would first be emailed to him for review. And because she would make this a private web group, only those who were invited to participate could log on.

Once Pastor Kevin had given his approval, the five of us discussed the girls' retreat. I had already called my grandparents and secured the cottage for the third weekend in June. Even though that didn't give us a lot of time to plan the event, everyone was anxious to kick off the new program as soon as possible.

For the next few weeks, we were all busy organizing the retreat and setting up the web group on the Internet. Before we knew it, we were at the cottage with the girls, having a great time relaxing by the river and swimming at the cove.

On Friday night, we assigned the girls to their small groups and had devotions together in the cottage's large family room. Before introducing *S.O.S. Online*, Cassie asked me to come up and share my experience at Tyler U.

Walking to the front, I sat down by the fireplace and invited the teens to gather around and get comfortable. As I paused to make eye contact with each girl there, a hush fell over the room.

"Very few people know what I'm about to tell you tonight," I began. "Let me start out by saying we all make mistakes in life. Some of them are small and easy to fix, but others are bigger and have more serious consequences.

"I learned the hard way that covering up mistakes opens a door for even more problems. As I look back on what happened to me, I realize that everything started when I made one compromise and agreed to do something I knew was wrong. That first little compromise led to a slightly bigger one, and then even larger ones followed. Eventually, the lies I told to hide what I was doing put me in a life-threatening situation. If it hadn't been for some good friends and the prayers of my parents, I wouldn't be alive to tell you how it all happened."

Taking a deep breath, I went on. "If you had known me in high school, you probably would've thought, 'Not Julia! She's a girl from church. She'd never do anything like that.' But I did. I didn't plan to, yet it happened anyway.

"I'm not proud of some of the things I've done, but I know God has forgiven me, and I've finally been able to forgive myself. I want to tell you my story because some of you sitting here think that nothing like this could ever happen to you. That's a dangerous attitude since that kind of confidence is pride. And the Bible warns us that pride will make us fail."

For the next hour, I told the girls about my experience living away from home at Tyler U. The girls sat mesmerized as I spoke. They weren't merely hearing a story; they were reliving each painful event along with me. By the time I was done, some of them were teary-eyed and others a little shaken, realizing just how easily they could be deceived, too.

In closing, I said, "I hope my story helps you to make better choices than I did. That's really what living a blessed life is all about—making good choices. God gave us His Word to study so we could make right decisions: ones that honor Him, bless us, and allow us to help others. And because He's a loving Father, He forgives us when we make mistakes. Then He helps us to get back on track to experience His very best for us."

When I finished, the girls broke into applause and pressed in around me, thanking me for sharing something so personal with them. Once they settled down, I turned the meeting back over to Cassie. She explained about the web group, how it was going to work and how the girls could remain anonymous by using a code name.

"I think you guys will really like this program," Cassie said as she wrapped up her talk. "You'll see that you're not alone, that other girls are feeling and going through the same things you are."

The teens all seemed excited about starting the web group, and the rest of the retreat flew by with a lot of fun and very little sleep. When I finally got back home late Saturday afternoon, I was exhausted.

Making myself a quick snack, I sat in the kitchen with my mom and gave her a brief recap of the weekend. By the time I finished my sandwich, I was ready to call it a day.

"I'm beat, Mom. I think I'll take a quick shower and crash. Don't bother to wake me up for dinner. I'll just see you in the morning."

"Sleep well, honey. Paul phoned earlier. If he calls back, I'll tell him you went to bed early."

"Thanks," I answered wearily as I collected my bags from the foyer and trudged up to my room. Too tired to unpack, I simply dropped my things in a corner and got into the shower.

Before going to bed, I checked my email. Karen had sent me a message announcing that she and Matt were engaged. I smiled and immediately sent a short reply, congratulating her.

"Well, at least my friends are getting engaged," I sighed as I crawled underneath my comforter. "Right now, I'd be happy just to *meet* my guy."

Reaching Out

After the retreat, Cassie, Danielle, Lindsay, and I got busy teaching the teens how to use the web group. At first, the girls had trouble coming up with code names, worried that the names they chose might somehow give them away.

Lindsay was the one who suggested they all use a different color shade. Being an art major, she came up with forty of them, like shimmering gold, dusty rose, azure blue, and so on. Then she put the names into a jar, and each girl picked one.

By the end of the first month, almost all the girls were participating in the weekly online sessions. They loved using code names to share their thoughts and feelings without any embarrassment.

In the beginning, the girls talked mostly about boys, school, and friends. I felt they were being a little guarded at first, sharing only minor concerns, testing the system to see if it was really safe to open up and tell something personal.

Then about six weeks into the program, Cassie received an email from a girl code-named Lemon Yellow:

> I can't believe I'm writing this to you. I'm afraid to say anything, but I've got to talk to someone. I'm just so scared. I'm out of control, and I need help, but I can't get help. If my mom finds out, it'll kill her. She's told me a million times that she couldn't deal with me getting into trouble like some other kids at school.

> I know when it all started. I wanted a boy in one of my classes to notice me, and he likes girls who are really thin. I've heard him say so lots of times. My mom likes to cook, and she's always after me to eat all the food and desserts she makes. One night after a big dinner, I felt totally fat and gross and got the idea to just go throw up everything. But I didn't. I ignored that impulse and went to my room instead.

> Eventually, that thought came to me after every meal, and I started looking at myself more and more in the mirror. Even though the scale read the same, I felt like I was getting fatter and fatter. I was constantly checking my clothes to see if they were getting tighter. Finally, I gave in to that voice in my head, and one night after supper, I stuck my finger down my throat and made myself throw up. It's been eighteen months, and I'm still throwing up. Only now, I'm taking laxatives, too.

I've tried to stop, but I can't. I can't go to my parents because they think I'm their perfect little girl and they'll both freak out! Can you help me?

Cassie immediately forwarded the email to me and the other leaders. After talking with Pastor Kevin, she sent a reply to the girl and asked if it was okay to share her story with the other teens. Lemon Yellow said *no*, that some of her friends in the group might already be suspicious of her and she didn't want them to know.

For the next two weeks, we all took turns ministering to Lemon Yellow online, trying to convince her to get help. We told her that hiding this problem would only keep her binging and purging, that her body would eventually break down from the abuse and she could die.

In one of my instant messages, I pointed out that her parents were the God-given authorities over her life, that she needed their love and support to get the professional help she needed. Even if they did freak out at first, God would give them the courage to face the situation and work through this problem with her.

Lemon Yellow was terrified to tell her mom alone. She asked if my mom and I could be there when she told her. She couldn't face her dad yet. I knew my mom would want to help any way she could, so I agreed for both of us.

It was then that the girl decided to reveal her identity.

It's me, Julia. Shelly Emerson.

My heart skipped a beat when I read Shelly's name on the screen. The Emersons had been close friends of my parents for years, and Shelly was right. Her mother *was* going to freak out.

I didn't reveal Lemon Yellow's identity to anyone but Pastor Kevin and my mom. Shelly had shared it in confidence, and there wasn't any reason why the other leaders needed to know. They were all just glad the girl had decided to work it out with her parents. But now that I knew who Lemon Yellow was, everyone in the web group had to draw a new code name.

After I talked with my mom, she prayed about the best way to get together with Shelly and her mother. We decided to invite them over for lunch the following Tuesday. Mrs. Emerson was the only one who enjoyed the meal that afternoon. The rest of us were uneasy, knowing the atmosphere out on the patio was about to change.

As planned, after lunch Shelly went inside the house to use the bathroom. My mom wanted to prepare her mother for what was coming. When there was a break in the conversation, she began by saying, "Madeline, there's a specific reason for this lunch today."

"Really?" Mrs. Emerson replied. "Like what?"

"Shelly has a problem she needs to tell you about, but she's afraid you won't be able to handle it."

"Oh Grace, Shelly's so dramatic. What could be so serious?"

"This isn't something trivial, Madeline. Shelly has a real problem, and you need to prepare yourself.

When she tells you, I want you to remember that *you're* the mother in the relationship; she's the child. You're going to have to set your feelings aside and focus on her and the pain she's dealing with."

My mom nodded at me, and I quickly left the patio to go get Shelly. When the two of us walked back outside, Mrs. Emerson immediately demanded, "What is going on here?" Shelly just stood there, head down, unable to look at her mom. Frustrated, Mrs. Emerson kept going. "Answer me, young lady! Tell me this big problem of yours right now!" Shelly dropped to her chair and started crying. Between sobs, she managed to tell her mom what she was doing.

"I don't believe it!" Mrs. Emerson exclaimed. "It can't be true. This couldn't be happening without me knowing about it." Turning to her daughter, she shouted, "If it *is* true, I want it to stop immediately, Shelly! Do you hear me?"

My mom broke in. "She hears you, Madeline, but do you hear her? She *can't* stop. She's tried repeatedly. It's no longer just a bad habit. She has an eating disorder, and she needs professional help."

Now Mrs. Emerson was crying. Holding her head, grieving, she said, "What did I do wrong? How am I going to tell Jack? No, I refuse to believe this. It's just not happening!"

My mom put her arm around her. "It took a lot of courage for Shelly to come here and tell you about this. She could've kept it hidden until it was too late to get help. This has been happening to her every day for the last year and a half; you just started dealing with it today. Everything's going to be all right, Madeline. Susan at church is a great Christian counselor, and she has helped many families work through things like this.

"Right now you need to stop thinking about how all of this will affect you and Jack and get Shelly whatever help she needs. Denying there's a problem or blaming each other won't accomplish anything. Only Pastor Kevin and our family know about this, and we promise to keep it confidential. Once Shelly gets better, she might want to share her testimony with other girls who are struggling with the same thing. Please, Madeline, be grateful your daughter is reaching out to you for help."

Mrs. Emerson was trying to pull herself together, but it was obvious she was overwhelmed. Seeing Shelly was hurt by her mom's reaction, I turned to her and said, "Look, Shelly, when I made all those wrong choices at Tyler, I thought I was only hurting myself. I forgot that my family loved me and had made sacrifices for me all my life, that it was only natural for them to be upset when they found out. So I had to give them time to work through the pain *they* were experiencing. I had to remind myself that my parents weren't vending machines, standing by to instantly hand out everything I needed. They were people with needs and feelings of their own. It took a crisis in my life to teach me that.

"I got into trouble when I stopped being truthful with my parents about what I was doing. That's when I moved out from under their protection, and it became easier and easier for the enemy to deceive me. That's what happened to you, too, Shelly. But now that you've brought all this out in the open, you can come back under your parents' guidance. Believe me; things are going to turn around for the better for all of you.

"Families need to be honest and transparent with one another. After my big mess up, my dad admitted something he'd been hiding from me all my life. He also took responsibility for what he'd done to contribute to my failure. Since that day, my dad and I have never been closer.

"I memorized a scripture to help me be upfront with my parents. It's James 5:16 in the New Living Translation: 'Confess your sins to each other and pray for each other so that you may be healed. The earnest prayer of a righteous person has great power and wonderful results.'"

Speaking those few words of Scripture broke the tension we all felt. My mom suggested we pray together, and by the time Shelly and Mrs. Emerson left that afternoon, God had already started the healing process. Mrs. Emerson had her arm around her daughter as they made their way to their car parked in our driveway. They were going home to tell Shelly's dad and help him work through his initial reaction.

Closing the front door together, my mom and I both let out a sigh of relief, glad the intervention was over. I gave my mom a hug and thanked her for being there for Shelly and her mother. We were both confident that with the Lord's help, the Emerson family would come out of this trial closer than ever.

First Kiss

The sultry August air hit me like a blast as I walked out of the air-conditioned Center to my car. Reaching down to open the door, I paused briefly to look at my reflection in the window. Rearranging some windblown curls, I frowned at myself and blamed the humidity for such a bad hair day.

Just then, I heard a car pull in behind me. Turning, I found Paul smiling through the open window of his silver SUV. "How's my favorite physical therapist doing?" he called out.

"Melting in this heat!" I exclaimed as I walked over to his car, still trying to keep my hair from flying all over my head in the wind. "What brings you here?"

"I just saw Brian, and we talked about going to a movie with you and Cassie tonight. You up for it?"

"Definitely. What time?"

"We'll pick you up at your place around seven thirty."

"Sounds great. Lucky you were passing by just now."

"Sure was," Paul laughed as he pulled away. From the look on his face, I knew luck had nothing to do with it.

Arriving home some fifteen minutes later, I headed straight to the shower to cool off. I'd had a frustrating session with a patient that afternoon and needed to relax. Before long, I was feeling better. Although I loved working in the therapy unit at the Center, I was emotionally worn out and looking forward to a weekend break. Once I had toweled off and slipped into some sweats, I quickly checked my email messages. Then, before taking a nap, I grabbed my Bible and read a few scriptures at my desk. Opening my journal, I wrote:

Father, I'm beginning to sense Paul has feelings for me. What do You think about that? I don't know what I think. We've been friends for a long time and always have a great time together. I know I've been wanting a boyfriend, but it's weird to think he could be the one I've been waiting for. At the moment, my life is pretty full with work and church, and school starts again soon. I'm happy with the way things are between us, but if Paul wants more, I'm going to have to make some decisions.

Maybe it's my imagination, and he just thinks of me as a friend. Probably not, right? Help me to know Your will and my own heart. I want to do the

*right thing and not just use him to meet a need in
my life right now.*

I closed the cover of my journal and then plopped
down on my bed, falling sound asleep in seconds.
The next thing I knew, a loud voice was waking me
out of a never-never-land dream. It took me a minute
to realize where I was, that my dad was calling for
me to come downstairs for dinner. Remembering my
date, I forced myself to get up and go join my parents
in the dining room.

An hour later, Paul showed up with Cassie and
Brian, and the four of us took off for the theater. The
movie was a spy thriller filled with nerve-wracking
scenes. The guys had to keep Cassie and me up to
speed on the plot since we had our faces buried in our
hands most of the time. Even though the story was
intriguing, we were both glad when it was over—too
much stress!

Once we got back to the car, Brian suggested a
drive to Murphy's Landing down by the lake. The days
were hot and humid during August, but the summer
nights were cooler, and it was an ideal temperature
to take a walk.

When we arrived, Paul and I separated from Brian
and Cassie and headed for a favorite bench where I
sometimes went after work to study and feed nuts
to the squirrels. I again had a treat for them in my
purse, but by the time Paul and I got there, all was
quiet. My furry friends appeared to be in bed for the
night.

Taking a seat on the bench, we talked for a while before Paul shared with me some of his plans for the spring. He'd been working part-time as a bookkeeper for a floral shop, and the owner had asked him to stay on after graduation.

"I'm thinking about accepting her offer, Julia. She's giving me a raise, and I can renew the lease on my apartment for another six months. I don't work tons of hours, so I'll have time to study for my CPA exam."

"Do you see yourself staying here in Weston for good?"

"No way! I only came out here because of my scholarship. As soon as I pass that exam, I'm going back to the West Coast. The weather's much better, and I want to start my own firm there. Last time I was home, I found the perfect place for an office down-town. My dad's already checking into it for me."

"Sounds like a great dream, Paul. God likes to give us desires and then help us make them a reality."

"Yeah, He sure does," he agreed, shifting his weight on the bench as he tried to find a more comfortable position for his long legs. "I'm getting tired of sitting, Julia. Let's take a walk out on the pier."

The moon was almost full that night as the stars played peek-a-boo with some scattered clouds drift-ing overhead. Paul and I slowly made our way down the long pier to a large deck that stretched out over the lake. We paused there to watch the ducks taking a late evening swim.

The night air seemed much cooler now, and as we leaned on the railing, Paul noticed I was rubbing my bare arms, chilled. Without asking, he took off his lightweight jacket and placed it around my shoulders.

Taken by surprise, I pulled the jacket tighter around me. "Thanks, that feels a lot better." Suddenly, I realized that the arm which had so thoughtfully placed the jacket around me was still there. I could feel Paul drawing me in closer to him as we continued to gaze at the lake and watch the city lights on the far shoreline.

"Feeling warmer now?" he asked with a gentle squeeze.

I shyly nodded that I did. *Maybe a little too warm,* I thought to myself. Feeling my face begin to flush, I hoped it was too dark for Paul to notice. In all the times we'd been together, this was the first romantic move he'd made.

Just by putting his arm around me, everything had changed between us. I felt it in my heart, and it was obvious by way he was looking at me. I didn't want to encourage him to go any further yet. I needed time to think. How did I feel about this change? What were my true feelings for him? I wasn't sure myself.

"Hey, you two. Enjoying the view?"

Paul and I both turned to see Brian and Cassie walking up to us. Their timing was perfect. Without knowing it, they had just rescued me from an uncomfortable moment.

"It's getting late," Brian pointed out. "You guys ready to take off?"

Everyone agreed, and we all walked back down the pier together. I instantly noticed that something had happened between Brian and Cassie. They were holding hands as they strolled along and couldn't take their eyes off each other. There was a glow on Cassie's face that said it all, and Brian was grinning like he'd just won an Olympic medal.

Wanting to pick up the pace, Paul and I passed them, taking the lead. I blushed again when he reached over and put his arm around me. I knew Cassie and Brian were watching, and I wondered what they were thinking.

Soon we were in Paul's car and on our way to take Cassie home. When we stopped in her driveway, she and Brian climbed out of the back seat. As they started toward the house, I lowered my window and light-heartedly called out, "Looks like the light finally turned green!"

"Yes!" Cassie gleefully answered back. "How about you?"

"Still yellow," I reported, giving her a final goodnight wave.

When Brian returned to the car, he asked, "What's all this green-light, yellow-light stuff? You two have some secret code or something?"

I grinned. "All girls have a secret code, Brian. Didn't you know that?" He and Paul just looked at each other and shrugged their shoulders.

Even though I lived only two blocks from Cassie, Paul took the long way around and dropped off Brian first. When we eventually got to my house, the lights were out, except for the one on the porch. Paul put his SUV in park and turned off the motor. "I'll walk you to the door," he offered.

We stood together on the front steps as I rifled through my purse, trying to find my key. Then I remembered it was still hanging in the mudroom where I'd put it after work. Fortunately, my parents always left a spare to the garage service door under a planter on the porch. Paul tipped up the pot so I could retrieve the key and followed me around to the side of the garage.

Opening the door, I flipped on the inside light and turned to say good night to Paul. Before I knew what was happening, I found myself in his arms, and he kissed me.

When our lips parted, he seemed as surprised as I was that he'd acted so impulsively. Still in his embrace, he drew me close to him once again and confessed, "I didn't plan that, Julia, but I'm glad it happened. I've imagined kissing you for so long, I guess I couldn't help myself. It's okay, isn't it? You wanted me to kiss you, didn't you?"

I wasn't sure what to say. "I'd be lying if I said I didn't enjoy that kiss, Paul. It's hard to spend as much time as we do together and not get involved. But I know from experience that two people can feel a strong attraction and still not be right for each other.

"You told me tonight that your heart's on the West Coast, that you want to eventually settle there. Mine isn't. I want to get married and raise my children here in Weston. I want them growing up knowing my parents and grandparents, going to the cottage with them in the summer. I just wouldn't be happy living anywhere else."

Paul wasn't about to let those objections stand in the way. "We don't have to decide anything tonight, Julia. I'm sure there's a way to work things out. My plans aren't set in stone. All I know is I care about you. Promise me you'll at least give us a chance, okay?" Before I could answer him, he kissed me again, affirming his feelings for me. Only this time, instead of returning his kiss, I cut it short and pushed away from him.

"What's wrong?" he asked, confused by my reaction.

"I just need a little more time to think this through," I explained, feeling pressured. "It would be easy for me to let you hold me and kiss me like this, Paul. I am attracted to you, but I don't want to start something that has no future. I think we need to step back and think before moving into the next stage of our relationship. Let's pray about us first and ask God what we should do. I don't want either of us to get hurt, and we could you know, so easily."

The next few moments were uncomfortably silent. I was the first to speak. "It's getting late, Paul. Let's say good night, and you can call me tomorrow, okay?"

I could tell he didn't want to pray about anything, that he already knew what he wanted. But he reluctantly agreed and wished me goodnight, squeezing my hand before walking away.

Stepping into the garage, I slowly closed the service door behind me and leaned against it, trying to process what had just happened. *Finally, a Christian man I am attracted to wants to be my boyfriend. It has happened at last. But what do I want? What does God want?* As I maneuvered my way around the cars and into the house, my head was spinning.

"How was the movie?" a voice asked as I walked through the mudroom and into the kitchen.

Startled at first, I surveyed the dimly lit room to find my mom sitting at the breakfast nook, sipping a mug of tea. "Oh, hi. The movie was okay I guess, a little intense. The guys loved it though." Grabbing a mug from the cabinet, I poured myself some tea and sat down across from her. "Why aren't you asleep?"

"I had a cappuccino late this afternoon with Madeline, and now I'm paying for it."

I shuddered a little. "Ugh. I still can't hear that word without feeling sick to my stomach."

Smiling, my mom passed me one of her oatmeal cookies. "I'll know you're healed from your Jay incident when I see you drink a cappuccino again."

"Well, that's the least of my concerns right now. I have more current issues to deal with."

"Like what?" my mom asked, taking another sip of her tea, suspecting what might be coming.

"I got kissed tonight. Twice, actually!"

"Is that so bad?"

"That depends on how you look at it. I really like being with Paul. He's a lot of fun and a Christian and so good looking..."

"So, what's the problem?"

"Oh, I don't know. I do want a boyfriend, but it seems weird that the one I've been waiting for all this time could actually be Paul. His feelings for me aren't casual, Mom. He's ready for a permanent relationship."

"And you don't feel the same?"

"Maybe, but I don't think we want the same things in life. He told me tonight he wants to go back to the West Coast and set up an accounting office there. He even has the place pictured in his mind. That's what's throwing up the caution sign for me, Mom. I feel like my destiny's here in Weston. I'm not sure how that's going to play out, but the Lord has plans for me here. He's keeping my heart fixed on that.

"I think Paul wanted to show me that he had a future before making his move romantically. That's why he told me about his plans tonight. And we've become so close, I don't think it ever entered his mind that I might not feel exactly the same.

"He was really surprised when I pushed away from his second kiss. When I pointed out that we had different visions, that I didn't want to leave Weston, he did an immediate about face and said his plans to go back home weren't definite. But I saw the look in his eyes when he was talking about his dream, and I don't think he's going to give it up and stay here permanently. He just said that because he doesn't want to lose me.

"You know, Mom, I've already been down this road with Jay. Paul's decided he wants me in his life, but he's not taking into consideration what *I* want and need. Now he'll probably be on a mission to get me to date him, to give him a chance and then eventually do what he wants. Even if by some miracle he did stay in Weston, he'd be compromising *his* God-given destiny, and I'd feel guilty for the rest of my life for stealing his dream."

"I'm proud of you, Julia. I don't know if you realize how much you've matured since dating Jay. You're taking time to think things through before letting your feelings dictate your decisions."

"Thanks, Mom. I understand that the longer you wait to break off a relationship, the harder it gets. Emotional ties get stronger with every date, and before you know it, you're in too deep to even *want* to turn back. That's when you start rationalizing that everything will somehow work out after you're married."

"Only it doesn't usually end up that way, does it, Julia? Most of the time, everything accelerates after marriage: good relationships get better and bad relationships get worse. I'm not saying Paul is a bad person, honey. He's a great young man and a committed Christian just like you. All I'm saying is that if a man isn't sensitive to your feelings now, he probably won't take them any more into consideration once you're married."

"That's just it, Mom. I understand enough about a Christian marriage to know that if Paul decided to return to the West Coast, I would need to adapt myself to my husband and go with him, even if I still wanted to stay here."

"That's how it works, Julia. But that's true no matter who you marry. You have no guarantee that any man will want to stay in Weston all your married life."

"I know, and when the time comes, I believe God will give me the grace to be happy living anywhere with my husband. But for now, I'm sensing that I'm supposed to stay right here. I think God had Paul share his heart with me before he kissed me tonight. That way I'd know about our different visions before romance swept in and carried us both away."

"I think you may be right, sweetheart. Pray about it before you go to bed, and see what the morning brings."

"Good idea," I responded with a yawn. "Bed sounds so good right now."

Both of us got up from the table and carried our mugs to the sink. As we made our way upstairs, I suddenly remembered something. "Oh, I almost forgot to tell you! I don't think I was the only one who got a first kiss tonight. Paul and I split up with Brian and Cassie for a while at the lake, and when we met up with them later, they were holding hands and had a *madly-in-love* look in their eyes. I didn't get a chance to talk to Cass alone, but I'll call her tomorrow and get all the details."

"Oh, I'm so happy for them, Julia. Those two have been in love for years. Your dad talked with Brian today—about being his preceptor and bringing him into the law firm eventually. Maybe that had something to do with his move forward tonight."

Arriving at the door to my room, I paused to kiss my mom good night. "That's great about Brian." Stifling another yawn, I added, "We can talk more about it tomorrow, Mom. I'm beat!"

"Good night, Julia. I'll pray about you and Paul before I go to sleep."

Chapter 15

Readjusting the Focus

Even though I was drained, I took some time and prayed about Paul before going to bed. I thought I heard the Lord speak two words before I fell asleep: *red light!*

When I woke up the next morning, I was certain God had told me not to date Paul anymore. When he called shortly after breakfast to ask me out again, I knew I had to tell him my decision. Although he tried hard to change my mind, I remained firm and made it clear we would just be friends from now on and only see each other at church.

Not having much of a choice, Paul reluctantly agreed to my request. But it was obvious that as far as he was concerned, the matter wasn't settled. I think he was hoping that after spending some time apart, I'd miss being with him and decide to give him a chance.

When I finally got off the phone, I sat for a minute and thought about what I'd just done. I was grateful God had given me the wisdom to stop things before either Paul or I got seriously hurt, but it was still a big loss. I'd been hanging out with Paul for more than a year, and it was fun to have a guy friend to do things with on the weekends. I would really miss him.

As I got up from the couch, I remembered something my mom had told me after breaking up with Jay. She said that long-term friendships with members of the opposite sex rarely stay the way they start. Often one person begins to feel something more than friendship, and the relationship must deepen or be redefined. The only consolation in my situation was knowing that the pain I was feeling now was a lot less in comparison to the pain that would be waiting for me down the road if I postponed the inevitable.

Later that afternoon I called Cassie, and she excitedly explained what had happened between her and Brian the night before:

> When you and Paul walked away, Brian and I headed for the music coming from the pavilion. On our way, he spotted a bench on the lawn and led me over to it.
>
> "Let's sit for a minute, Cass. I need to talk to you."
>
> "All right," I said, sitting down. "Is something wrong? You sound so serious."
>
> "Nothing's wrong; I just have something important to tell you, that's all. We've been friends since we were in middle school, Cass, and it's

been a great friendship. But I don't want to be friends anymore."

I couldn't believe what I was hearing. Suddenly, my heart was struck with fear, and I knew at that moment that I loved him more than I'd even admitted to myself. Blinking away tears, I asked, "Can you at least give me a reason?"

Seeing my reaction, Brian immediately reached over and took my hand. "I didn't mean that the way you took it, Cass. What I meant was I can't go on being just friends. I feel so much more for you than that. But if that's all you want from me, we'll have to stop seeing each other. I'm in love with you, Cass. I have been since we were kids, and now I need to know how you feel about me."

He stopped and waited for my reaction, looking both hopeful and afraid at the same time. "Don't you know, Brian?" I laughed in relief, squeezing his hand. "I've loved you from the very start."

Brian slowly let out the breath he'd been holding in until I answered. Hearing that I loved him, too, he couldn't help but scold me a little. "Then why didn't you tell me all these years? You must've known how I felt!"

"I did know, Brian. But I also knew you wanted to be a lawyer more than anything, that we had a long wait ahead of us before we could even think about getting serious. Are you sure we're still not getting ahead of ourselves? You have law school to finish, you know."

"Are you kidding? We've waited long enough. You'll be teaching somewhere next fall, and Julia's dad has offered to bring me into the firm when I finish law school. We talked about it this afternoon in his office. It was knowing what I could offer you that gave me the courage to tell you how I feel."

"It's finally happening, isn't it, Brian?"

"Yes, and you've been worth the wait. I just want to know one more thing."

"What's that?"

"Can I finally kiss you?"

I nervously smiled and nodded, and Brian gently pulled me close to him. He briefly looked into my eyes before leaning down and giving me the kiss we'd both been dreaming of.

When Cassie finished her story, I squealed with delight. Her time had finally come, and I told her how excited I was for her. Then I shared what had happened between Paul and me. She understood my red-light decision, and although she was sorry it wasn't my time yet, she was proud of me for doing what I thought was right. We talked for another half hour before finally saying goodbye.

As I hung up the phone, I realized things weren't going to be the same between us. Brian was Cassie's best friend now, and that's the way it should be when you're in love. We always knew it would happen someday, and that day had arrived.

Fighting feelings of self-pity, I went to my room and kneeled by the bed to pray. *"No matter how lonely or left out of things I feel right now, Lord, I'm not going to feel sorry for myself. I'm sure I'm making the right decision about Paul and me. You've already confirmed that in my heart. There's always a cost attached to doing the right thing, but You reward us for every sacrifice we make to obey You—beyond anything we can think, hope, or imagine.*

"It's time for Cassie to be in love with her Mr. Right, and I'm going to be happy for them. My time hasn't come yet, but I have the assurance from Your Word that it will happen for me in Your perfect timing. I'm feeling that it's getting close, maybe because I turned twenty-one last month, or maybe it's just wishful thinking.

"Anyway, I sure hope You're letting my Mr. Right know just how much I'm going through for him. This must be some guy You have planned for me! I can't help but wonder if he's suffering a little for me, too. Please continue to mold me into the woman he needs me to be for him.

"Character development isn't much fun, is it? Sorry! That sounded a lot like complaining, didn't it? Enough of that! Thank You, Father, for hearing my prayer, in Jesus' name."

Classes were starting up again in three days. I would be back to studying, and with the girls' group and my work schedule at the Center, I had more than enough to keep my mind occupied. By readjusting the focus on my present priorities, I continued to trust God for my future.

Once school began again, the teens in our web group started to open up more than ever. Danielle received an interesting email from a girl code-named Passion Pink—a name which, ironically, matched her subject matter. Submitted as a hypothetical question rather than a personal admission, her email was titled: *Is it really sex?*

Some of the girls at my school are doing things with boys that they say isn't really sex because they can't get pregnant. Well, actually the guys are the ones telling them that. I'm embarrassed to even be asking this, but I really want to know.

When are you having sex, anyway? Does that mean actual intercourse? How far can you let your boyfriend go before it's considered sexual activity? A lot of guys don't want to date you unless you touch them or let them touch your private parts. If you can't get pregnant, is doing that stuff wrong? Can you still get AIDS and other diseases by just messing around like that? I hope you know what I'm talking about. I really don't want to come right out and say it. Can you answer my questions?

When Pastor Kevin's wife read this email, she immediately called her friend Justine, a medical doctor and lecturer for a well-known abstinence group. She was more than qualified to answer Passion Pink's questions. Justine was asked to type out a response that could be posted with the original inquiry for all the girls to read online. This is what she wrote:

> Dear Passion Pink,
>
> Please don't think that you're alone. Most girls want answers to the very questions you've raised, but they're afraid or embarrassed to ask. Let me start out by answering your first question: Is it really sex? The answer is absolutely!
>
> When you're making contact with a guy's sexual organ, that's sexual activity. Likewise, when a guy is touching your private areas, you're having sex with him even though that will not cause you to become pregnant.
>
> You asked if you could get diseases from what you called messing around. Again, the answer is absolutely! You might be surprised to learn that there are more than twenty different sexually transmitted diseases (STDs). They can be passed through the vagina or anus, or through oral sex. Some can even be passed through skin-to-skin contact such as intimate touching or kissing, as in French kissing.
>
> Common STDs include gonorrhea, HIV, hepatitis B, chlamydia, syphilis, genital herpes, and HPV. Many of these diseases are incurable and can ruin your ability to have children in the future or lead to cervical cancer.
>
> You said that the guys were the ones saying that what they were asking their girlfriends to do wasn't really sex. After reading what I just told

you, these guys either don't know what they're talking about or they're just a bunch of liars.

If so, what else are they lying to you about? How many sexual partners have they had besides you? I've counseled with many a girl who is suffering from an STD, yet her boyfriend swore to her that he'd never had sex with any other girl, that she was the only one. Because she believed him and gave him what he wanted, she's daily reminded of her bad decision.

Girls who have been recently diagnosed with an STD are often sent to me for counseling, most of them crying, "This isn't fair! I didn't know my boyfriend was lying to me!" That's the point, girls! There's no way to know if a guy's been sexually active before you, so be determined to say NO when he asks for sex.

You said that boys don't want to date girls who won't do what they want sexually. I've answered your questions, so let me ask you a few things. Is having some guy pay attention to you so important that you're willing to risk ruining your life to give him what he wants? Are you really worth so little? He obviously thinks so. Regardless of what he tells you, he doesn't love you; he's just using you. When he's finished with you, he'll most likely move on to someone else.

The only way to prevent getting an STD is by abstaining from all sexual activity until you're married. If you want to confirm that this is true, or if you would like to learn more about STDs, you can contact the Center for Disease Control online at www.cdc.gov. They have a lot of helpful information and can direct you to other websites as well.

Here's something to think about. You may be having sexual experiences in secret now, but if you contract an STD, all known cases have to be reported. Then you won't be able to hide the truth anymore.

Here's something else for you to consider. Premarital sex not only threatens your health physically; it can cause great damage to your emotional health as well. I can't begin to count the number of heartbroken girls I've counseled who continue to struggle with issues long after those wrong relationships have ended. Because of the emotional intimacy shared with an old boyfriend, a girl often feels used or betrayed, making it difficult for her to trust anyone else in the future.

My advice to the girls I counsel is to make God your first love. He will never hurt you or leave you and always wants the best for you. Confess your past mistakes to Him and ask for His forgiveness. Then start making better choices and be determined to wait to enjoy sex within the safe boundaries of marriage.

From my studies and counseling experience, I can say with confidence that there are no real advantages, spiritually, emotionally, or physically to engaging in premarital sex. I hope I've answered your questions and that you'll make good choices, ones you won't regret for the rest of your

life. Always remember how much you're worth!

Justine Keller

When the girls read Justine's report, they were grateful that someone had the courage to bring up this subject. Several of them sent in their reactions:

"I knew these things were going on, but I didn't have anyone to talk with about them."

"My boyfriend keeps bugging me about doing some of the things Justine talked about. I finally see him for what he really is—a jerk! I broke up with him last night."

"Funny, I never realized how much my self-worth depended on my popularity with guys."

"No guy is touching me unless he commits to me for a lifetime and marries me!"

"It happened to me. My boyfriend talked me into doing things I knew were wrong. At the time, I just wanted to make him happy, but the guilt I felt afterwards was horrible. I'm not dating him anymore. I've asked God to forgive me, and I've made the decision to wait for marriage to have sex again. I wish I could forget what happened, but I can't. He told his friends what we did, and they won't let me forget."

We had a leaders' meeting after the girls' responses were posted. This was exactly what we'd been praying for: open and honest discussions. In fact, Justine's reply gave us an idea for even more discussions on a variety of subjects. We could post other young women's stories on the web page and let the girls respond to them afterwards.

Lindsay's college roommate had a sister who wanted to share her story, and after it was approved, it was posted for the girls.

Lost Angel

I was not very popular with guys in high school. In fact, I had very few dates. Because of that, I felt inferior to the girls who always seemed to have a boyfriend. I started to feel bad about myself, afraid that nobody would ever want me.

That all changed when I went away to college and started getting a lot of attention from one of the international students. He was a computer science major from Iran and so different from the guys I'd known in high school. Habib was great to talk to, and he seemed genuinely interested in me. He was really good looking, and he had a way of making me feel beautiful for the first time in my life. He was very nice to me and appeared to have good moral standards as a Muslim.

Because I was afraid of never finding anyone to love me, I pushed aside my concerns about getting involved with a man from a different culture and religion. We got married in the middle of my sophomore year and moved into a small apartment off campus. I got pregnant right away.

It didn't take me long to realize that I'd made a big mistake. Habib totally changed after we were married. All the charm he had used to get me into the marriage quickly disappeared. My needs and opinions no longer mattered to him now that I was his wife. Our marriage was anything but happy.

When our daughter was about three years old, I couldn't take it anymore. I left him and filed for divorce. Despite my protests, the judge gave him overnight visiting rights two times a month.

Almost half a year later, it happened. Habib picked Fatima up around eight on a Saturday morning to take her to the zoo with some of his friends and their children. He was supposed have her back no later than four o'clock the next day. When he still hadn't shown up by six, I panicked, sensing that something was wrong. I tried calling his place, but there was no answer.

Desperate to find my daughter, I got into my car and drove to his apartment. Nobody was there. I went to another apartment where some of his friends lived and pounded on the door until one of them answered. Over his shoulder, I could see two other men in the living room. When I told them why I'd come, they just stood there, looking at me.

"Where is my daughter?" I shouted at the top of my lungs.

Glaring, Razin sharply replied, "Where you will never see her again. Habib took her back to Iran where she belongs. You won't be able to find her, so go home! There's nothing to do." Then they all laughed in a way that still frightens me to recall. They didn't see anything wrong with what Habib had done.

I immediately went to the authorities, who made every effort to help me, but everything eventually led to a dead end. I didn't know much about Habib's family in Iran, and because he had such a common last name, tracing him was next to impossible. Besides, as Habib's daughter, Fatima was technically a citizen of Iran, too, and our government didn't have many options.

I can't explain what happened inside me the moment I realized I would never see my daughter again, never hold her in my arms, and never watch her grow up. I knew my little angel was lost to me forever.

Months later, I joined a support group to help me cope with my depression. It was in those meetings that I learned how many other women were in similar situations. A lot of their husbands had only married them to get a green card. I will never forget my daughter, and for the rest of my life, I will deeply miss her. Please learn from my mistake.

Jeanie

When the girls read this story, they were furious. Three common responses were:

"I can't believe something like this could happen!"

"How could he get away with that?"

"Isn't there any way for Jeanie to get Fatima back?"

Realistically, the only answers we could give the girls were:

"The only people who know where Fatima is are Habib, his family, and his friends, and nobody's telling. This little girl is now somewhere in Iran, far beyond the reach of her mother. Even if Jeanie knew where her daughter was and flew there hoping to see her again, she probably couldn't legally leave the country with Fatima without the father's consent. That would mean using illegal means to get Fatima back, putting everyone's life at risk."

"Let us be clear, girls, so you don't misunderstand. Things like that happen to women in the United States all the time, not just by husbands from another culture, but by estranged husbands in general. We didn't share this story with you because God would never match you up with a Christian man from another country or culture (even though that has its challenges). We're just letting you know that marrying a man from a different religion or set of values is a legitimate risk. And unlike this woman who shared her story, we want you to choose your husband carefully and marry him for the right reasons."

As the days and weeks passed, the activity within the web group accelerated, and I could see that, at least for now, God was using me in the lives of these teens. The free time I'd been spending with Paul was being replaced more and more with my online ministry.

It had been almost four weeks since telling Paul I didn't want to see him outside of church. That was easier said than done, however. It seemed like I was always bumping into him around town, in the singles' group, or at the campus café, where we'd sit and have a cup of coffee together.

I was really trying to keep the no-dating line drawn, but I didn't want to be rude or hurt Paul's feelings, either. It was hard to resist sitting and talking with him sometimes; I did miss being with him.

After one of those chance meetings, I sent up a quick prayer on the drive home. *"Father, being single may be a necessary part of life, but it's full of complications. When I finally meet my Mr. Right and know he's the man for me, I think I'll do cartwheels! Thanks for being my first and most important love, in Jesus' name."*

Shortly afterwards, I started to become good friends with one of the older teens in the web group. A Christian from the time she was small, Angela was smart and interesting, and I liked getting her ideas for subjects that the other girls would want discussed in the web group. Angela said two things in particular were problems for girls her age: feeling ugly sometimes and feeling unimportant or insignificant without a boyfriend.

Because I had experienced those emotions myself in the past, I posted online the beauty lessons my parents had taught me. I also wrote out the version of the Cinderella story that Jen's mother had shared. I even threw in the example of *Amy's glasses* so the girls could see that too much focus on yourself can cause you to feel like the only one going through things.

When I told my sister-in-law what I was doing online with the teens, Jenny suggested the leaders put their old school pictures on the site for the girls to view. At first, Danielle and Lindsay refused to do it; they said it would be too humiliating. But Cassie and I eventually talked them into it, and each of us posted at least one unattractive photo from our teen years. We hoped the pictures would help the girls to see that ugly ducklings *can* develop into lovely swans.

The responses to those stories and pictures were amazing. The girls could see that much of what they were experiencing was common to all girls their age. They were starting to realize that the enemy speaks the same negative thoughts to everyone's mind and that they just had to resist those thoughts, believing God's view of them instead.

Although I loved seeing how the web group was changing the girls' lives, it was taking up a lot of my free time, and I really needed a break, even if just for a weekend. Fortunately, I'd been invited to Gretchen's wedding downstate, and I was looking forward to seeing some old friends again.

It didn't seem that long ago that I'd introduced Gretchen to Gary at Tyler, and now they were getting married. Funny how things work out. My dad was a little worried about my traveling alone to the wedding, so I invited Angela to go with me.

Driving several hours, the two of us arrived at Gretchen's hometown and checked into our hotel. After dinner and some fun at the pool, we stayed up late in our room, laughing, talking, and painting our nails. Finally, we decided to be sensible and call it a night.

It was exciting to see my Tyler friends the next day at the wedding. The ceremony was so beautiful that Angela and I both had to wipe away tears. I briefly congratulated Gretchen and Gary at the church, but we didn't have a chance to really talk until the dinner later that evening.

At the reception hall, Angela and I sat at the same table with Kenny, Karen, and Matt, catching up and reminiscing about our Tyler days. Having heard the story about Jay, Angela felt like she knew everyone already. We all had a great time, and the night was over much too soon. Once more, I had to say goodbye to my friends, not knowing how long it might be before seeing them again.

Back in my hotel bed that night, I reflected on the past few hours. So many of the people closest to me had already met their match from the Lord. Cassie had Brian, Gretchen had Gary, and Karen had Matt. Kenny and I had no one, so far. We were both in dating limbo, still waiting. Suddenly a feeling of hope swelled within me, and I knew I was next. I just had to be...

Risky Business

Checking my email, I saw I had a new message. I clicked on it expectantly, only to see it was from the University, confirming my schedule for spring classes. I sighed, thinking how long the last semester had felt without Paul. Even though I hadn't changed my mind about going out with him, I did miss being with him. I still saw Cassie a little on the weekends, but she was with Brian most of the time. And that *sure feeling* I had of meeting Mr. Right at the start of the semester? It turned out to be just an unreliable feeling. To my disappointment, I hadn't met anyone even close to dating material.

Suddenly, another email message popped up on my screen, interrupting my pity party. It was from one of the girls in the web group. Opening it up, I couldn't tell if Aqua Marine was relaying a friend's problem or really talking about herself. She wrote:

I have a friend who's into some stuff on the Internet. She's meeting a guy online and talking to him about sex. She says he doesn't know who she is because she didn't give him her real name. I told her what she's doing is wrong, but she just laughed and said it's only a game, that lots of girls do it. She said it wasn't really wrong—just a fun way to mess around without getting into trouble.

Is it wrong? They're not actually touching each other. I know what Justine Keller said, but my friend can't get pregnant or an STD by just typing words.

What do you think?

Unsure how to answer, I forwarded the email to Pastor Kevin. He called Justine and got a referral to a woman who had just gone through something like this with her daughter. She posted the following story:

Deadly Games

This is written to you by a mother who, until two years ago, had no idea what was going on in chat rooms all across the country. Like many parents, I thought my daughter was just using the Internet to talk to friends or do homework. Then I noticed Tina was starting to spend more and more time in her room. I wasn't alarmed because I trusted her and figured she was just working on school projects. I had no idea what was really going on until it was too late and she had totally disappeared.

I will never forget that Friday night. My daughter told me she was going to the mall after school with her friend, that she wanted to spend some of her Christmas money on new clothes. I didn't even know Tina was missing until later that evening. I was worried when I hadn't heard from her by seven, so I called her friend's house to see if they were over there. Marissa answered the phone, and her words still echo in my head every time I try to sleep. "I haven't seen Tina since school let out today, Mrs. Lacey."

Instantly, I knew something was wrong. Tina had lied to me. Why? Where did she really go? Where was she now? I begged Marissa to help me—to tell me something, anything that might help me find my daughter. She and Tina were close; surely Tina had confided in her about where she was going. No, Marissa said she didn't know anything.

I felt so helpless. There was nothing I could do but wait. When Tina hadn't come home by eleven, I called the police. I didn't know what else to do. I had already called the local hospitals and all of her other friends. Nobody had seen or heard from my fifteen-year-old daughter, including my ex-husband. The police told me to come to the station in the morning if Tina hadn't come home by then.

She didn't come home, and I filed a missing persons report the next day. One of the female officers asked me if Tina had been having any problems at home. Could she have run away?

That thought had never crossed my mind. I knew she was missing her father since our divorce, but she seemed to have adjusted to our separation fairly well. Maybe she'd been hurting more than I'd realized, holding it all inside.

I called Tina's father again from the police station, and he immediately left work and came down. Neither of us could give the authorities any leads. Tina seemed to have vanished into thin air. Her friends and teachers all said she was acting normally at school on Friday. Nobody had seen her since.

Frantic for clues to find Tina, I went home to her room and started going through all her things. I found nothing. Finally, I sat down at her computer and got into her email. What I found was beyond my ability to believe: emails and replies to emails that were nothing short of verbal pornography. Tina had been corresponding online with a guy she called Manny. He was seducing her, and she was teasing him with sex talk.

I eventually learned from Marissa and a few of Tina's other friends that many of the kids at school were doing this. It's called cybersex. "Nobody means anything by it," they said. "It's just a game we like to play with these guys for fun. We don't know who they are, and they don't know our real names, so it's safe."

The last email Tina received from this Manny said, "Meet me at the mall after school Friday. I want to see if you're as sexy as you sound. You know the place we talked about. I'll be there at four. Look for a guy in a blue football jersey."

I printed off a copy of the email and took it down to the officer on the case. She said it looked like Tina had been abducted. "I'm sorry to have to tell you this, but it does happen. Girls think these guys are harmless, but often they're professional predators looking for girls to exploit.

"Sometimes these men snag girls who are lonely and looking for a boyfriend to talk with in a chat room. There's actually no sex talk involved in those cases. The girls think they're corresponding with boys their own age, but these are not teenagers they're talking to. They're typically much older guys who are experienced at getting inside a girl's head and making her believe whatever it takes to trap her. If your daughter went with this Manny, and it looks like she did, chances aren't good that you'll ever see her again.

"Girls start out thinking this is a harmless game, but for many of them, it turns out to be a deadly one. They end up in some sort of sexual exploitation or in the morgue."

It's been a little over two years now, and there's still no trace of Tina. I don't know if my daughter's even alive. I have nightmares thinking about what might be happening to her if she is alive.

I have little hope of helping my daughter anymore, but maybe by sharing my story, I can help you avoid Internet predators. In addition to your own safety, consider your parents, how they would feel if you suddenly disappeared.

Not knowing what happened to Tina torments me. I still watch for her out the window and rush to the phone every time it rings, praying it might be her. When it isn't, my heart breaks all over again. If I knew for sure she was dead, I'd at least be able to grieve and go on. But this way, there's no closure. Each day begins with hope and ends with disappointment. Nobody should have to live like this. It's like dying every day.

Mrs. Lacey

When this story was posted on the website, three girls from the youth group admitted to having online relationships with boys they'd met in chat rooms. None of their parents knew they were meeting online with them.

Because of that, we decided to post another story from a woman Danielle had met through a friend at Weston U. She had just made it through something we thought the girls should hear.

Narrow Escape

I'm in my early thirties, and it seems like I've been in school forever. But in order to do what I feel the Lord has for my life, I need to have my doctorate. My studies are very demanding, and I've had to sandwich in some work time periodically during this academic journey. That doesn't leave a lot of time for serious relationships. I did have a boyfriend a few years ago, but for me, it wasn't love. It was settling, and I didn't want to settle for someone just to have a guy in my life. Eventually, we broke up because I couldn't commit to him the way he wanted to commit to me.

Months later, feeling lonely, I got into a chat room, looking for a boyfriend. I was being careful, though. I only used chat rooms for Christian singles. I connected with a man who lived in another state, and we started emailing. We both had big aspirations, shared many of the same interests, and seemed right for each other from the very start.

Soon we were exchanging pictures and setting up a meeting in person. Two weeks later, each of us drove half the distance, and we met for dinner. Although we stayed in the same hotel, it was all very innocent. We made sure our rooms were on different floors and spent most of our time at restaurants or in a private section of the lobby. After one weekend of being together, we felt we knew enough about each other to get engaged. We had talked for hours about all the things it usually takes couples months to discover.

I had never wanted a big wedding, and in the excitement of the moment, we almost eloped the next weekend. But after thinking it over, we decided to have a small ceremony later that month. Chad quickly arranged for me to meet his parents, and then I introduced him to mine. They seemed to like Chad, but they weren't happy that we were getting married after knowing each other for less than a month.

I felt I knew everything I needed to about Chad to make that decision. He had shown me his bank records, revealing a substantial savings, and he gave me his pastor's phone number so I could verify his character. He had already bought a beautiful diamond ring, keeping it in reserve for his fiancé when he became engaged one day. He gave it to me in the most romantic way, and I was sold. Chad appeared to be what any girl would want.

The next week I called one of my close friends, excited to tell her how Chad and I had met and that we were getting married. She wanted to be happy for me, but she was concerned that I was rushing into marriage with a stranger. I argued that we had talked together at length and that we matched up well. I also pointed out that I was getting older and might not have another opportunity like this one.

"Time is your friend, Karleen," she reminded me. "Can you really know a person after just a few weeks? I mean, think about it for a second. You're committing to marry him. That means being together for the rest of your life. Don't rush this. Get to know him better first. Find ways to see him in person more often. You aren't necessarily getting the whole picture by talking with him on the phone or the Internet. It's too easy to be fooled that way. He can pretend to be anyone he thinks you want him to be. It's not that easy to fool you if you're with him around his family and friends because you can see how he reacts to people, how he handles different situations. If he really is the great guy you think he is, time will reveal that, too, and you'll be just as happy."

I will be forever grateful I took her advice. After talking to her, I saw that she was right and I needed to postpone marrying Chad. It wouldn't hurt to take some more time to get to know each other better. I realized we were both acting a little too desperate and rushing into getting married.

A few months later, I began to see a side of Chad that I would not have believed possible. When he was visiting me at my apartment, I got a phone call from my old boyfriend. He was having a problem and just wanted to talk to me. After a few minutes, I told him I was engaged and that it wasn't appropriate for him to call me anymore. Chad overheard the conversation, and I thought he would be proud of the way I handled the call. Instead, when I hung up, he flew into a jealous rage and began to attack me verbally. He accused me of terrible things and used profane language that absolutely shocked me. I had never heard him talk that way before.

That started an ongoing pattern in our relationship. He always apologized after one of his outbursts, promising it would never happen again. Only it did, repeatedly. Eventually, I found out Chad had an anger problem he'd been dealing with for some time.

I broke our engagement, but he kept contacting me, trying to make me believe he was in counseling and getting better. He had a way of making me feel sorry for him, making me feel guilty for not giving him another chance. Because I still had feelings for him, I did give him another chance—more than once. But the problem was recurring, and he never did get better. I finally came to see that he was good at manipulating me, that the only way for me to be free of him was to cut off all communication, which I did. I'm thankful he lives in another state or things could've been worse.

I'm telling you my story so you won't make my mistake and get involved with someone you shouldn't. If you're not spending time with a guy one on one, it's easy to be deceived. I shudder to think of what life would be like for me now had I actually married Chad.

Karleen

After Pastor Kevin found out that some of the girls from the youth group were in chat rooms, he asked me to find some programs that screened Internet sites. Then he held a meeting with the teens' parents and urged them to protect their kids from the wrong kinds of online influences. Mrs. Lacey's story helped some of them to see how important it was for them to safeguard their home computers.

When I got back from that meeting, I went to my room and looked up a verse I thought of during the presentation. Jumping online, I went to an online concordance and read the verse in a few different translations. I especially liked 2 Timothy 3:6-7 in the New Living Bible.

The subtitle of the chapter was *The Dangers of the Last Days,* and the first five verses prophesied about some of the people who would be living during that time. Then verses 6 and 7 read:

> "They are the kind who work their way into people's homes and win the confidence of vulnerable women who are burdened with the guilt of sin and controlled by many desires. Such women are forever following new teachings, but they never understand the truth."

"Isn't that what we're seeing today, Lord?" I prayed. *"People are working their way into our homes through certain TV shows, movies, and Internet sites. Instead of 'vulnerable women,' another translation says 'silly women.' That could easily apply to young girls. And these things are happening to our boys as well through the violence and pornography that many of them are watching.*

"Please help the parents of our teens to wake up and take the steps needed to protect their homes. Growing up today involves some risky business; kids need their parents' attention more than ever. May the teens receive what their parents are doing with gratitude, knowing it's being done for their protection and because they're valued and loved."

Once I'd finished praying, I quickly got ready for bed. Just before falling asleep, I tacked a P.S. onto my prayer. *"Kiss my guy for me, Father, wherever he may be, and tell him that I love him already, in Jesus' name."*

Staying Strong

Winter was finally over, and spring was here again with budding trees and colorful tulips. This was my favorite season because it always brought with it hope for new beginnings.

I could hardly believe I was already into my eighth semester of college. If I hadn't lost one term's worth of credits when transferring, I'd be graduating in a few short months with Cassie. I regretted losing those credits, but there was nothing to do now but make the best of it and finish my degree in the fall.

Things seemed to be changing all around me in the lives of the people I knew and loved. Cassie was student teaching at an elementary school in our area, and when she wasn't in class, she was busy preparing for the next day. We still saw each other at church, of course, but when Cassie had free time on the weekends, it belonged to Brian.

I would often catch myself watching the two of them in church on Sundays. The love they had for each other was obvious, and although I was thrilled for Cassie, I had to fight being a little envious. The frustration of waiting for my Mr. Right surfaced now and then, usually late at night, right before bed. In those moments, I'd turn to God and journal for a release.

Father,

I know You've heard all this before—not just from me, but from every woman who's still a lady in waiting. But it helps at times for me to vent a little. You know what I'm thinking and feeling, so there's no sense pretending. I so much want a guy of my own to love. Sometimes I ache to feel his arms around me, even though I don't know who he is. I'm taking the advice Jen's mom gave her and trying not to picture him. Only You know what he looks like. I don't want to be so zoned in on a certain type that I miss him when he finally shows up.

*It's funny the little things that trigger envy. Like yesterday in church when Flip introduced his new girlfriend to all of us. I couldn't believe that even **Flip** has a special someone in his life. And who do I have? Nobody!*

I was instantly ashamed of myself for thinking that. Melody is a sweet person, and I'm certainly not interested in Flip myself. He really has become a transformed man, thanks to the time Pastor Mark spent with him. I hear he's doing really well

in his business courses, and I am happy that this other part of his life is being fulfilled as well.

I've been tempted lately to start dating Paul again. He still wants to go out, and we have so much fun together. I know he's not my Mr. Right, but at least I won't be lonely while I'm waiting...

Sorry, Father. That would be completely selfish and really unfair to Paul. I apologize for even thinking that way. But please give me some credit. It's not easy to keep resisting a guy like Paul— especially when he's fun and good-looking, and I want a boyfriend so much.

***HELP!!!** I need some extra grace here, Lord. I keep busy during the week, but Friday and Saturday nights are hard. Somehow curling up with a good book doesn't make things better.*

*Okay, enough grumbling. It's only making me feel worse. Instead, I'm going to start praising You for all the blessings I **do** have. I choose to thank You for the good things in my life right now instead of focusing on the one thing I want and don't have yet.*

Thanks for understanding me and letting me cry on Your shoulder for a few minutes. My time is scheduled to meet my Mr. Right, and he is coming. I know that from all the Scripture promises I have taped to my mirror.

Please don't feel bad. Even though I'm longing for him, You're still my first love, Jesus.

Fortunately, these surges of emotion didn't last long, and I was able to shake them off and get back into my schoolwork, job, and online ministry.

One night while I was studying for semester finals, I took a break and checked my email. There was only one message, from Shelly Emerson. She said she was doing well and that her purging had completely stopped. She went on to say:

> I believe I'm finally free of this thing and that it's time for me to tell my story online. I talked it over with my parents, and they agree. I'll write it out and send it to you this week for review. I learned in counseling that lots of girls my age are fighting eating disorders and that only a certain percentage of the ones who receive treatment get better. I also found out that the sooner you get started, the better your chances of recovery are. If my story can encourage girls to get help as soon as possible, then I want to share it. I'm not ashamed anymore to admit I had a problem. All I want to do now is help other teens.

I typed a reply to Shelly, telling her how proud I was of her. I thought about Gary and Gretchen and how they had overcome the mistakes they'd made at college. They would both applaud Shelly for using her past struggles to help others heading down the same wrong road.

Shelly kept her promise, and her testimony was approved and posted online for all her friends to read by the following Friday. None of the girls in the youth group had even suspected she'd been battling bulimia.

One of Cassie's girls came to her a week later and confessed that she was experiencing some of the symptoms Shelly had mentioned. The girl agreed that her parents needed to know, and once they were told, they got her into counseling right away. After only a few sessions, she was doing better and was grateful she hadn't waited to get help.

By now, I was receiving frequent emails from my girls saying how much the web group was helping them think and seek godly advice before making important decisions. It was nice to be making a difference in their lives, even though my social life was suffering from it. Not to mention the fact that for the past two semesters, I'd been working almost thirty hours a week at the Center while taking my college courses at night.

Now that exams were over, Cassie was busy preparing her résumé and going on interviews, looking for a full-time teaching position for the fall. Brian was home for the summer, working at my dad's law firm. When they had free time, they naturally spent most of it together. I understood, but it didn't seem like summer without my best friend to run around with all the time.

To my disappointment, two of my final classes weren't going to be offered in the fall semester, so I had to sign up for the June session. Between work and school, I had little opportunity for fun in the sun. My only consolation was that time was passing quickly, and the frenzy of activity was distracting me from the painful fact that there was still no romance in sight.

Meanwhile, my friends Karen and Matt had just gotten married and were taking a mission assignment in Spain. Wanting to save the expense of a big wedding, they had decided on a small ceremony with family only. I sent them a gift of money, knowing they couldn't take much with them abroad.

I also sent Kenny a short email since he still wasn't dating anyone. I really didn't expect an answer from him, as he wasn't much for writing. But I knew Karen had told him about the wedding, and I wanted to console him a little, even though I was actually feeling frustrated myself.

Before I knew it, it was July, and my brother emailed saying that the project in Chile had been extended and he wouldn't be bringing his family home for at least another year. Although we called each other on Skype a lot, it wasn't the same as seeing him in person. I missed both John and Jenny terribly. I was also anxious to hold my little niece, who was just now turning three.

This was probably the hardest summer I'd ever had. It certainly wasn't like the fun-filled ones I'd enjoyed in the past. I felt like one thing after another was trying to discourage me. Finally, the Saturday night before the school term was about to start again, something happened that was almost too much for me to bear.

My parents had gone to a concert that evening, and by seven-thirty I was ready to get out of the house myself for a while. Feeling a little lonely and restless, I decided to drive down to Benny's and get the sundae I'd been craving all day. The singles from church usually met up there on the weekends, and I figured I would find someone I knew to sit with— maybe even Cassie and Brian. They stopped in there a lot.

Cruising past the restaurant, I saw that the place was packed out, forcing me to find a parking space on a side street and walk back to Benny's. Sure enough, when I came through the front door, I heard a voice calling to me off in the distance. Standing up to be seen more clearly, Cassie motioned for me to come join her.

After making my way through a maze of crowded tables, I gave Cassie a brief hug and greeted Brian seated next to her. Turning, I saw Paul sitting across from them in the booth. Grinning as though he were both surprised and happy to see me, he immediately got up so I could sit down. Then he quickly scooted in beside me. Their food was just arriving, so I ordered myself a hot fudge sundae—minus the whipped cream.

"Cutting calories, are we?" Cassie teased as she dipped one of her fries into a heaping glob of ketchup on her plate.

Coming right back at her, I said, "Well, not every-one has your metabolism, you know. You're up to five, or is it *six* meals a day now?" That solicited an *ooooooh!* from the others at the table, and it felt like old times—the four of us kidding and laughing together, the way it was before I stopped going places with Paul.

Later I found out why Cassie hadn't called me to join them that night. Brian had already invited Paul, and Cassie knew I wouldn't want to come with him there. She respected me for sticking to my decision to stop seeing Paul, knowing that some girls would've just used him until the right guy came along. She admired me for refusing to be like that. Saying *no* for the right reasons was definitely costing me now, but saying *yes* for the wrong reasons would end up costing Paul even more later.

Nevertheless, that night I didn't put up my guard or try to analyze relationships. I just had fun with my friends for the first time in a long time. Cassie was celebrating the start of her first teaching job the following week, and everyone was excited for her.

After a while, Brian checked his watch to see we'd been talking for over an hour after finishing our food. Not wanting to tie up our booth any longer, we decided to leave. Paul grabbed my check, but I quickly snatched it back, taking him by surprise. "Thanks anyway, Paul, but I'd rather you didn't."

Brian shot Cassie a *none-of-our-business* look, and they quickly slid out of the booth to go pay their bill at the counter. After some further arguing about my check, Paul and I caught up with them. Although Paul triumphantly held both checks in his hand, I was quite unhappy about it.

When we all got outside the restaurant, we said our goodbyes, and Brian and Cassie took off, leaving

Paul and me in awkward silence. "I'm...I'm...parked on a side street down this way," I finally stammered. "See you tomorrow at church, Paul."

"I'll walk you to your car," he insisted, placing his hand on the small of my back, skillfully guiding me to the inside of the sidewalk. I was only parked a block away from Benny's, but the trip to my car felt much longer as I tried to make conversation. Eventually, we meandered off the main street and headed for where I was parked on Woodmere Drive.

I tried hard to ignore the strong romantic vibes Paul was sending my way as he walked close beside me, reminding myself that I only had to make it to my car just ahead. When we got there, I nervously fished my keys out of my purse and unlocked the door.

As I turned to say good night, Paul pulled me up toward him and kissed me. It wasn't like the two kisses we shared the previous summer. This one was a much deeper kiss, one he'd been saving up and couldn't hold back any longer.

Caught up in the moment, I didn't fight against him. Instead, I found myself surrendering to his embrace and returning the kiss. When I realized what was happening—what I was doing—I quickly pushed him away.

"No, Paul. We can't do this. Nothing's changed since last summer. We're still two people who are attracted to each other but wanting different things in life."

"Listen to me, Julia," he answered, drawing me into his arms again. "I love you. Don't you understand that?" Pulling back just enough to look at my face, he smiled and gently stroked my hair. "I know you love me, too, but you're so hung up on where we'd live if we got married that you're not being fair to either of us. Give me a break, will you? I just can't believe your concerns are enough to keep us apart."

"That's the trouble, Paul," I responded, stepping back to distance myself from him. "Now, it's your turn to listen. You're so hung up on what *you* want, you're not even hearing what I'm saying. I don't believe God's putting us together as a couple. It's not just about you and how you feel about me. *I* have to think we're right for each other, too. If God really wants us to be together, why do I sense so much resistance?"

Paul just stood there, shaking his head and looking at me with both love and disbelief. He was apparently too frustrated to answer my question, so I tried to explain further. "Do you think refusing you is easy for me, Paul? Well, it's not. I want to be in love just as much as you do, but I'm not going to get into a relationship that can't be permanent. I'm not going to date you just because I'm tired of waiting. I'm not going to do that to you or to me! One of us has to keep our head."

"So you're saying there's no hope for us. Well, I don't believe that, Julia. There's more between us than you're willing to admit. Maybe our love didn't happen overnight, but it did happen, and it's real. Remember the first time we ran into each other at the mall?"

I nodded.

"Right after that, we started going places together outside of church. At first, I wanted the same thing from our friendship that you did—no commitment. For me, it was just fun to have a pretty girl to hang out with. My focus was on getting through school, and you made being friends easy because you didn't ask for anything more.

"I'm not sure when I knew I'd fallen in love with you, Julia, but it was months before I kissed you. I told Brian, and he warned me to take it slow. He told me about a bad experience you'd had with some guy from Tyler, that you were still healing and really guarded. The last thing I wanted to do was scare you off, so I took his advice and waited for the right time to tell you how I felt.

"The drive we took down to Murphy's Landing last summer was planned, Julia. Brian had decided he was finally going to tell Cassie that he loved her. I felt like it was time for me to move forward with you, too. We figured a walk down by the lake would give us the perfect setting to talk to you and Cassie. I was still a little worried, but Brian encouraged me to go for it. We both know how badly that turned out for me."

Listening to Paul's confession, my heart felt like it was breaking. Unable to speak, I just looked away from him, trying to hide the tears that were now slipping down my cheeks.

Paul gently raised my chin so he could look into my eyes again. Seeing my tears, he tenderly wiped them away as he offered, "Look, Julia, if you need more time, I'll give you more time. You'll be starting fall classes soon, and I've finished setting up the new system at the floral shop. Now that everything's up and running, I'll have time at night to study for the CPA exam in May. All I'm asking for is a chance to date you on the weekends. I just want to be with you, all right?"

"No, Paul, it's not," I was finally able to reply. "If you're hanging around Weston thinking I'll change my mind and leave with you once you've passed your exam, you're wrong. I asked God about us last summer, and He gave me the red light where you're concerned. I'm sorry, but unless I hear differently from Him, that's just the way it has to be. The sooner you're able to accept that, the sooner you'll start looking for someone who can return your love. So let's stop arguing and just say good night, okay?"

"You know what I think?" Paul asked, visibly upset. "This red-light thing of yours is just a cover up. The trouble with you is you're afraid to fall in love again, with anyone. I feel like I'm paying for what your old boyfriend did to you!"

I was trying so hard not to cry, I couldn't defend myself. I just stood there, tight-lipped, refusing to answer. Seeing I wasn't going to respond, Paul finally threw his hands up in frustration and walked off.

Once he was out of sight, I turned and got into my car. As I pulled into traffic, tears began streaming down my face. I frantically grabbed a handful of tissues and dabbed away the tears so I could see to drive. After what seemed like forever, I finally rounded the corner to my house.

When I pulled into our empty garage, I was relieved my parents weren't home yet. I desperately needed to talk to someone, but the only one I wanted was my Lord. After closing the garage door, I went inside and ran up to my room. Falling to my knees beside my bed, I began to pour out my heart to God in prayer.

"Father, I'm so miserable right now. I believe I did the right thing tonight, but it hurts to do the right thing. When Paul kissed me, I lost it for a few seconds because I'm longing for my mate just like he is. You were there with me; You know what happened. Paul's a great guy, and even though I don't think he's Your choice for me, it felt good to be in his arms. I enjoyed being kissed. He looked so handsome in that orange shirt, and he was even wearing the cologne I love. The trap was set, and because I was lonely and a little melancholy when I left home, I fell in.

"Thank You, Lord, for helping me come to my senses in time. I don't want to encourage Paul in any way or care for him even more myself. That could happen all too easily. I can see how a girl can settle for the wrong guy when the right guy isn't anywhere in sight. I always thought of 'wrong guys' as guys with issues. But sometimes there's a nice guy like Paul who's still wrong for you. That type of guy is the hardest to say no to, especially when he's trying to win you over. I'm thankful my friends aren't pressuring me to give in to Paul. That would make resisting him even harder.

"I'm not telling You to hurry up, Lord. I'm just being perfectly honest. I'm feeling a lot of pressure lately

about not having a boyfriend, much like my first year at Tyler. I talked to my grandma about it last weekend, and she told me it was a good sign—that sometimes when a person is trusting You for something and the pressure of waiting seems almost unbearable, a break-through is near.

"I hope she's right. But while I'm waiting, please help me, Lord. Help Paul, too, so he can put closure on his feelings for me. I don't want to go through anything like this with him again. It's too hard on both of us. Give him all the grace he needs to pass his CPA exam in May. Then show him that there's nothing here for him so he can go back home and start building his dream.

"I need to confess something, Father. When Paul accused me of being afraid to love again, those words shook me a little. What if I didn't hear You accurately last summer? Am I denying my true feelings for Paul? Is he right, and I'm holding back because of what hap-pened to me with Jay? I don't think those things are true, but if I've been wrong, please show me Your will and redirect me in a way that's unmistakable. Until then, I'll continue to heed the red-light warning I believe I received from You a year ago.

"Thanks for being with me every minute of the day and night, Lord. Staying strong isn't easy. I need Your grace to stick to what I think is right when facing temptations—to experience the joy that comes from being in Your presence—a joy that isn't dependent on having everything I want. Please look into my heart and know just how much I love and appreciate You.

You're wonderful! I trust You completely and pray these things in Jesus' name."

By the end of my prayer, I was completely spent. I quickly washed my face, brushed my teeth, and slipped into my favorite pajamas. Crawling between the sheets, I tried to read my Bible, but my eyes were so tired and swollen from crying, the words were starting to blur. Reaching over, I switched off the lamp on my nightstand and flopped back down onto my pillow.

"I hope my eyes aren't puffy for church in the morning," I sighed before turning over and drifting off to sleep.

Chapter 18

Ups and Downs

Much to my dismay, my eyes were still a little puffy the next morning. Enough so, my mom noticed and asked me about it during breakfast. My parents both listened as I explained what had happened between Paul and me the night before. They did their best to encourage me that the time to meet my Mr. Right was coming soon. But I wasn't very consoled. It's hard to be optimistic when you're feeling so frustrated.

It didn't help matters when Paul sat through the entire church service that morning with his head down. I didn't get much out of the sermon because I was fighting off the waves of guilt that kept sweeping over me. When I couldn't take it any longer, I flipped to the back page of my notepad and wrote:

I refuse to feel guilty about Paul! I <u>will</u> <u>not</u> allow his disappointment about me to change my mind.

I've never been anything but honest with him. If he stays unhappy because I won't date him, that's his choice. I am not responsible!

As time passed, the tension between Paul and me gradually lessened when we saw each other at church. I was hopeful that he'd finally realized there was no romantic future for us.

Just about the time I was starting to feel better about Paul, another situation popped up to threaten my peace of mind. Don McNulty was conducting a class again in the same building where I was taking one of my P.T. courses. He hadn't been at Weston U since I took his Ethics class more than a year earlier. The rumor around school was that he'd been doing a lot more traveling for business—no time for teaching. That had been a great relief, but now he was back on campus again, and I was trying my best not to run into him.

Yet that is exactly what happened just before winter break. Knowing McNulty was teaching on the opposite end of the floor where I was taking an evening class, I had managed to avoid him all semester by deliberately using the east stairs coming and going. That way, I was nowhere near his room. My plan failed, however, shortly after a Thursday night lecture. Hurrying out of the women's bathroom, I wasn't watching where I was going, and the two of us accidentally collided.

"Well, if it isn't Miss Duncan," the professor immediately responded, stooping down to pick up the two books that had slipped out of my arms and onto the floor. "Lovelier than ever," he added with a smirk as he straightened, his eyes indecently scanning me up and down.

I read his intent, and a sick feeling hit me in the pit of my stomach. Totally out of character for me, I didn't answer him. I just reached out, took my books back, and quickly walked away, losing myself in a group of students leaving down the east stairway.

As I approached the top of the staircase, I heard McNulty calling to me above the noise of the crowd. Or was that just my imagination? I wasn't sure. Panic struck me as I envisioned him following me, and I virtually raced down three flights of stairs to avoid any further contact with him, my heart beating wildly as I weaved my way through the mass of exiting students.

When I reached the first floor, someone grabbed my arm and stopped me. "Hey, Julia—what's wrong?"

Startled, I turned to see Flip looking down at me. "Boy, am I glad to see you!" I gasped, trying to catch my breath.

"You okay?" he asked, concerned. "You're tearin' down these stairs like you're runnin' from a ghost or somethin'."

"Not a ghost, just someone scary."

"Huh?"

"Never mind. I'll explain some other time. What are you doing here? You graduated last spring, remember?"

"Yeah, can you believe it? I'm what you call an *alumnus* now. I just came by to pick Melody up from class, and then we're goin' to get somethin' to eat at Benny's."

Just then, Melody walked down the stairs and joined us. "Hey, Julia," she said as she shifted her backpack to the other shoulder. "Sorry I'm late, Flip. My professor asked to see me for a minute after class, but then he disappeared. I got tired of waiting and left. I'm glad he didn't come back; he kind of gives me the creeps for some reason."

"Let me guess, Melody. You're talking about Don McNulty, right?"

"How did you know?"

"It's a long story. How about I meet you guys at the restaurant? There's something I need to tell you about him. But could you walk me to my car first? I'll explain why when we get to Benny's."

"You got it," Flip replied.

I was grateful to have my friends with me as I walked out into the night air. It was darker than usual that evening. Or maybe it just seemed that way because I was still unnerved by my run-in with McNulty. As the three of us walked on the sidewalk that fronted the building, I looked up and saw a man standing before a window on the third floor, looking down. Although I couldn't identify the man, I was sure it was the professor watching me leave.

Flip and Melody delivered me safely to my car, and we were all sitting in Benny's fifteen minutes later. While we were waiting for our orders to arrive, I explained about how McNulty had tried to hit on me, past and present. Flip was furious when he heard, ready to go start a fight. Once Melody and I got him calmed down, we came up with a more reasonable idea.

The professor had been paying some special attention to Melody lately, so we were afraid he might pressure her the way he had me, just before the final exam for his class. Since the test was scheduled for the following week, Melody only had to be in his classroom three more nights. The plan was for Flip to go with her each time. If McNulty wouldn't allow him in the room, he would just wait for her outside in the hall.

"I hope that loser starts somethin'," Flip sputtered. "I'd like to belt him, just once. What he's doin' isn't right. Somebody needs to turn him in."

"If he hits on me again, I will," I assured him. "But McNulty didn't do anything tonight I could actually report. It wasn't so much what he said; it was the way he looked at me and made me feel. It's like his sexual innuendos are conveyed more with body language than with words. What he's communicating is pretty clear, but it's difficult to prove."

With that, Flip got mad all over again, and we had to calm him down a second time. Afterwards, I left for home, only to have pretty much the same reaction from my father when I told him.

"What a jerk," my dad muttered in disgust. "Don McNulty has no professional ethics, yet he's teaching an ethics class. That's pretty sad. If that man comes anywhere near you, Julia, pushing himself on you or anyone else you know, I want to be told about it.

He shouldn't be teaching if he's sexually harassing students."

Fortunately, that evening I had attended my last class for the semester in that building. My final for the course was a research paper, and I simply had to drop it off at my professor's office.

Now I just wanted to put the whole incident behind me and enjoy the feeling of accomplishment that comes with earning a Bachelor's degree. It had seemed like such a lengthy undertaking, but I was finally done with this stage of my education and ready to start my graduate work immediately after Christmas break. I'd picked up my class schedule that morning, and none of my night classes would be in the building where McNulty was teaching.

Relieved that everything had worked out, I said a prayer of gratitude as I got ready for bed that night. I'd already spent time reading my Bible before class, so I pulled my comforter up around me and was sound asleep in minutes.

The holiday season was always a big event in our home—lots of fun and tons of work and preparation. Huge boxes were brought up from the basement each year to decorate the house inside and out, and every room smelled of freshly-baked pies or cookies.

Once everything was decorated, our family liked to sit around the fireplace at night, roasting marsh-mallows and chestnuts over an open flame, the only lights coming from the hearth and Christmas tree. I loved these quiet moments with my parents.

Best of all, my grandparents were staying in Weston during December this year. They rotated between our different relatives' homes during the holidays, and this was the year for them to spend Christmas Day with our family.

As it turned out, this Christmas was especially sweet for me. My love tank was definitely running on low, and I ate up the extra affection I was receiving from my family. I had to admit I was getting drained from my shifts at the Center and the time I was investing in my web group girls.

Church, work, and school seemed like an endless treadmill, and I was starting to feel as if I'd been put on a shelf and forgotten. Then there was the added stress of feeling bad about Paul, not to mention the McNulty issue. At times I wanted to shout, "Hey, Mr. Right! I know you're *somewhere* out there. Stop taking so long to find me!"

My vacation was speeding by with New Year's Eve only a few days away. Our singles' pastor had planned a formal dinner for us at a nice restaurant, but I didn't want to go. I knew Paul would be there, and as lonely and frustrated as I was feeling, I'd probably run into his arms if he came anywhere near me. I might even find myself engaged to him before I knew what hit me! No, it was a lot safer staying home.

"Lord, help me to remember that this stage of my life is temporary. This is only one New Year's Eve out of a lifetime of celebrations. Someday, I'll be ushering in the New Year with the man I love, and I'll be free to return his kisses without any reservations. Is it

possible that all this could happen by Saturday night, Lord? Just thought I'd ask. It never hurts to dream!"

I helped Pastor Mark with some of the arrangements for the singles' dinner but stuck to my decision to stay home that night. My parents went to a dinner party at the Emersons' house, and although I had been invited as well, I didn't feel like going. Instead, I rented a romantic movie and settled into the family room with a soda and a huge bowl of popcorn. Just as I was drying my eyes from the final love scene, the doorbell rang.

"Oh, great," I moaned. I was in such a romantic mood from that movie, I knew I was a goner if it was Paul at the door. Peeking out the sidelight, I was relieved to see Brian and Cassie standing on the front stoop.

"Am I glad to see you two!" I cried as I opened the door. Grabbing their hands, I almost pulled them into the foyer. "What a great surprise! Go on in and sit down in the family room," I instructed as they slipped off their coats and laid them over the dining room chairs. "There's some popcorn on the coffee table. Help yourselves. I'll get some sodas from the kitchen and be right there."

When I returned with a glass in each hand, Brian and Cassie looked as if they were about to burst. "Hey, what's up with you two? You can't be this happy about bringing in the New Year with me." I had been so excited when they arrived that I hadn't noticed Cassie's hand. She was wearing an engagement ring.

Brian couldn't wait any longer. "Want to see what came with dessert tonight?" he asked, holding up Cassie's left hand for me to see.

"Oh my gosh, Cass. That diamond's amazing! It looks just like you. Did you pick it out yourself?"

"No, Brian surprised me," Cassie answered with a giggle.

With tears in my eyes, I gave each of them a hug. "I'm so happy for you guys. When's the big day?" I asked, shoving the popcorn bowl aside so I could plop down on the coffee table directly in front of the sofa where they were sitting. "Have you picked a date yet?"

"He just asked me a couple hours ago, Julia," Cassie laughed. "We'll figure out a date soon, but it definitely won't be this summer—probably the summer after. My *husband-to-be* wants to be practical and finish law school before we get married. That's okay; it'll give me more time to save for the wedding. You know my parents don't have a lot of money to spend on a big ceremony."

With his arm around her, Brian leaned over and gently planted a kiss on Cassie's cheek. "I don't care what kind of wedding we have as long as I marry you."

The three of us sat talking until I noticed it was almost midnight. "Time for a toast," I announced. Walking to the refrigerator, I took out a chilled bottle of sparkling grape juice and pulled out three champagne glasses from the china cabinet in the dining room.

Returning to the family room, I poured the bubbling liquid into the glasses and passed them to my friends. Lifting my glass, I said, "To Brian and Cass on the night of their engagement. May your life together be filled with happiness, and may you love and appreciate each other even more in the years to come." As we clinked our glasses together, the hall clock began chiming out the old year. "Happy New Year!" we cried out in unison after it struck for the twelfth time.

We talked for a few more minutes before Cassie explained that she and Brian needed to get going. Brian's parents were at her house celebrating, and they wanted to get there and tell their families the good news before the party broke up.

After seeing them to the door, I straightened up the family room and headed upstairs. Sitting at my desk, I pulled out my journal and wrote:

Thank you, Father, for a friend like Cassie. We've been close for years, and now we get to share the most important moments of our lives. When this night started, I was feeling sorry for myself and needed to feel special and loved. I did when Brian and Cass came over and shared their engagement with me before anyone else. Thanks for giving Cassie such a wonderful man to love her.

Dare I ask, Lord? Am I next? Am I even close to being ready?

After a minute of listening without an answer, I figured I might as well go to bed and get some rest. I lightheartedly reasoned that tomorrow might be the day to meet my man, and I wanted to look my best.

After washing off my makeup, I looked in the mirror and asked, "Does everyone have as many ups and downs in life as I do? I wonder..."

Internal Affairs

The following days passed quickly, and winter break was over—time to start grad school. The first few weeks were demanding, but I loved what I was learning and could see how this part of my education was going to help me with some of the more difficult cases at the Center.

Going to grad school while working didn't leave me much free time, but my busy life was actually a blessing—less opportunity to feel lonely. Meanwhile, the web group size was growing, and two new leaders had been added. Marcy and Jolene had ten girls in their groups as well.

A psychology major, Marcy was really good at counseling the girls on difficult issues. Jolene had come from a very dysfunctional family and proved that no matter how bad your home life was, you could experience a wonderful turnaround when you surrendered your life to Jesus.

Pastor Kevin invited Jolene to tell her story online to the web group, and she agreed. Unaware of the details, the girls were all shocked when the story was eventually posted. Even the other leaders were surprised, including me. None of us knew what a painful childhood Jolene had experienced. She titled her story ***Getting Help:***

> My story isn't unique. There are countless girls all over this world who have lived through the nightmare of sexual abuse, often by a family member or friend of the family.
>
> I don't remember my father; he left my mother right after I was born. I only remember living with my stepfather. He was an alcoholic, and for years, he sexually abused me. After each incident, he threatened to hurt my mom if I told anyone. So I grew up trapped in an environment of fear and shame. Truthfully, I didn't want to tell anyone because it would've been so humiliating to have people know.
>
> When I was in middle school, I met a Christian girl named Alesia, and we became friends. She invited me to come with her to church, and my mom let me go. It was there I began to learn about God and how much He loved me and wanted to help me. Only I couldn't believe it at first. Finally, I got up the courage to ask the Sunday school teacher, "If God loves us so much, why does He let bad things happen to us? Why does He let people hurt us?"

The teacher explained to the class that God isn't controlling the choices people make. He's given us all a free will. But because of that, we can easily make mistakes that lead to bad situations or even become the victim of someone else's bad choices. Then she said that God's kingdom in heaven and on earth operates under authority to keep order. Authorities were designed by God to protect us. But because authorities are made up of people and some people aren't following God or His ways, they can use their authority in a wrong way and hurt the very ones they're supposed to be protecting.

Then she said something that changed my life. She said that when an abuse of authority happens, the only way that a hurting person can be helped is by telling another authority, like a parent, teacher, or police officer. If the person is too afraid or ashamed and keeps it secret, the abuse will go on since no one else knows anything bad is happening. She said that God really loves us and wants to help us, but He needs us to cooperate with Him by being brave enough to tell the truth.

That day, I accepted Jesus as my Savior and Lord. It was also when I realized that if I wanted my stepfather to stop sexually abusing me, I had to tell someone. I started with my mother. Her reaction showed that she already knew what was happening but was too scared of my stepfather to do anything about it. She begged me not to say anything to anyone else.

The next day when my mother was at work, it happened again. Now that I was a Christian, something rose up on the inside of me, and I resisted my stepfather's attack more than ever, leaving me with several bruises and abrasions. When he was finished, he left me in tears to go out drinking again. I cried out to God, asking Him what I should do.

My first thought was to call Alesia. I reached for the phone next to the bed and dialed her number. Her mother answered, and between sobs, I explained to her what had happened and that I needed help. She told me to stay where I was—not to get out of bed—that she was on her way. Before leaving her house, she called 911.

Alesia's mom arrived just ahead of the police, and she went with me when I was taken to the hospital for an examination. Because my step-father's attack on me was so recent, they were able to gather conclusive proof that I was being sexually abused at home. God took it from there, and I never spent another night in that house.

After a bunch of legal red tape and a few months of staying in juvenile care facilities, I was eventually placed with a loving Christian couple. The Ashtons went to the same church as Alesia's family, and after hearing about my situation, they immediately applied to become my foster parents. Two years later, they legally adopted me.

People who know my story have asked how I dealt with being separated from my mother,

even though I was undoubtedly glad to be rid of my stepfather. My answer to that question is complex and has definitely evolved over time.

Of course, I initially missed seeing my mom. Children love their parents, even if they aren't doing everything they should. It's just a natural attachment kids feel. Still, I was so happy to finally be in a safe, caring home with the Ashtons that I gradually adjusted to not seeing my mother.

I found out later my mom never wanted to see me again anyway. She blamed me for getting my stepfather into trouble with the police and was more than willing to allow the Ashtons to adopt me. After I graduated from high school, I learned that my mom had eventually divorced my jailed stepfather, remarried, and moved up north. One of my favorite verses in Scripture is Psalms 27:10 because it says, "When my father and my mother forsake me, then the LORD will take care of me."

Believe me; I know what it feels like to be forsaken by father and mother. But there's more to being a parent than biological reproduction. It's the love and care you give a child that entitles you to be called a parent. In my heart, the only real mom and dad I've ever had are my adoptive parents.

When I received Christ in that little Sunday school room at Alesia's church, God gave me a new life. And when the Ashtons took me into their home, God gave me the two loving parents every child needs and deserves. Unfortunately, not every child living in an abusive home experiences the same happy ending I did. Most abused children are too afraid to tell anyone that they're being hurt. In my case, a friend introduced me to Jesus, and the message of His love and forgiveness gave me the courage to tell the truth to the right person at the right time.

I'm finishing my degree this semester and going into social work back home. I know there are kids out there who need to be rescued and put into homes with caring parents like I was. God has called me to do that work.

Please understand that I talk about my past whenever I get the opportunity to help others, but I'm no longer controlled by it. Jesus has healed me from past hurts because I've chosen to forgive those who hurt me, knowing they were probably deeply wounded themselves as children.

None of us gets to pick our parents before we're born. We're all a product of someone else's decisions. Some kids are birthed into loving families, and others find themselves in abusive homes. My children won't be able to choose their family, either. That's why I'm going to make sure I marry God's choice for me so we can allow Him to help us be the parents our children need for a safe and happy life—to be used as a relational bridge leading each of them into a close relationship with the Lord.

I want to tell my story to girls like you who, I believe, already have good parents, to help you fully appreciate and thank God for them, knowing

that the few restrictions they put on you for your safety are really acts of love.

Also, for those of you who never knew your mother or father and were adopted by a loving family, get down on your knees and thank God for them, too. You have no idea what kind of an abusive home situation you were rescued from. Instead of feeling rejected, embrace the people who are raising you. They're your real parents.

Stop and think about this: the teenagers you're trying so hard to please and think are so important now are probably people whose names you won't even remember in the years to come. Remind yourself that your friends have not lived any longer than you have, that they don't know much more than you do. They haven't invested in your life since you were born or sacrificed anything to give you a good home. Your parents have, and they'll continue to invest in you until the day they die.

After hearing my story, I've had a lot of girls tell me that they didn't realize just how blessed they were to have such great parents. Not perfect parents, of course. Just great ones. Hopefully, my story has helped you to come to that realization, too.

As always, I feel the need to conclude by making an appeal. Should you or anyone you know be experiencing abuse at home, sexual or otherwise, please get help! Silence is the abuser's only protection. The truth is your only salvation! These situations usually don't get better without professional help. They only get worse. Feel free to come to me or any of your leaders if you need to talk to someone.

Jolene Ashton

A few weeks after her story was posted, one of the girls, code-named Taffy Cream, sent a message to Jolene online, telling her about abuse in her home. It turned out to simply be poor communication between her and her parents regarding friends and privileges. Jolene was able to help Taffy see that she was adding to the problem with her negative attitude toward her parents. She told Taffy:

> You're not always going to agree with the rules your parents make concerning your life. But God expects you to obey your parents anyway, as long as what they're telling you to do doesn't contradict Scripture. The years that you're living with your parents aren't just to meet your needs materially and emotionally; those years become a training ground for you to learn to submit to authority.

> Kids sometimes want to break away from their parents' authority so they can be truly free. But there's never going to be a time in your life when you can just do whatever you want without regard for anyone else. You're always going to have to answer to someone else's rules, like those of your teachers, pastors, and employers, not to mention all the civic laws you'll be required to obey.

Let me give you a tip that may help, Taffy. Many times we don't feel like doing what the authorities in our lives ask us to do. God understands that the natural side of us doesn't always enjoy doing what's right. We have a tendency to be pretty self-centered. We prefer things that are comfortable and fun for now; plus, none of us really enjoys waiting for what we want to have or experience. Fortunately, God considers the big picture and is more interested in what is going to benefit us in the long run.

The process of growing up into a mature believer in Christ is a lot like dying to your selfish wants a little every day as you surrender to His will. Dying to self is definitely uncomfortable, but you have to die before you can have a resurrection. That's what I want more than anything—to live a powerful, resurrected life now, while I'm still here on earth.

Try to remember, Taffy, God never promised us we'd always be happy with people and circumstances. What He did promise us was a joy unspeakable that comes from knowing and obeying Him, strengthening us to face whatever we're going through with people and circumstances. I'd rather have constant joy instead of just periodic happiness. How about you? The choice is yours!

Jolene posted the conversation she had with Taffy Cream for the other girls in the web group to read. It not only ministered to them, but to the leaders as well, including me. Actually, this was the *second* time Jolene's words had really touched me.

The first was when Jolene shared her story online. For days after that, I found myself giving my mom and dad more than the usual dose of affection. Every time I looked at my dad, gratitude flooded my heart for how honorably he'd always treated me, how he'd been affectionate with me without making me feel uncomfortable. Jolene's story had brought a much greater appreciation to my heart for both my mom and dad and the way God had helped them to raise me.

The advice Jolene had for Taffy Cream struck another chord in my heart. I saw that I was beginning to fall back into the same obsession to have a boyfriend that I'd experienced before meeting Jay. Remembering the disaster my obsession had caused the last time, I was determined to reflect a little more now—before it was too late.

I knew that the Bible encourages Christians to examine themselves, so that's exactly what I did. I asked myself why this was happening again, what was really going on in my heart. I knew something was changing because, in a way, it felt like dying.

Based on what Jolene had shared about dying to your own wants and surrendering to God's will, I wondered if my desire to be in love was starting to get out of balance. Would I somehow have to die to self before I could actually experience my heart's desire? Searching for answers, I wrote out a prayer in my journal:

Father, search my heart and help me to understand what's going on here. On one hand, my relationship with You has never been stronger. On the other hand, my mind is frequently under attack about still having to wait to meet my Mr. Right.

I'm ashamed of myself for the way I really felt when Flip and Melody announced their engagement last Sunday at church. Even though I smiled and congratulated them, I felt jealousy rush through me. It's not that I wasn't happy for them. I was. But I was jealous because the waiting was finally over for them but not for me. I could almost hear my heart cry out, "Why would You do that for them, Lord, and still make me wait?"

Wow! Now that I write that down, I can see something. Is it possible that I feel I've done more to deserve being engaged than they have? I guess that's spiritual pride, isn't it? Sorry, Lord. Please forgive me.

None of us deserves anything from You based on our works. You love all of Your children impartially, and I know my time is coming, too. I really believe that, Lord, so why are these old, anxious feelings resurfacing again?

As I finished writing that last sentence, the Holy Spirit reminded me of a familiar scripture. I didn't know exactly where it was, so I reached for my concordance. I found the verse in Acts 1:7 and read it.

"And He said to them, 'It is not for you to know times or seasons which the Father has put in His own authority.'"

I meditated on that verse for a minute. Then I realized that Jesus was answering a question His disciples had just asked Him in the previous verse: "Lord, will You *at this time* restore the kingdom to Israel?" Jesus answered that the timing for things was solely the Father's business. Then He went on to explain in the next verse where their energies needed to be focused instead: on being a witness for Him to the world while waiting for the promised event.

I started writing again:

The whole time I was in high school, I envisioned having a boyfriend at college. So when I went away to school, I neglected my responsibilities as a Christian and became a poor witness on campus because my focus was on finding a boyfriend instead of on my relationship with You.

Tell me, Lord; am I feeling frustrated lately for the same reason? Have I subconsciously set up a time-table for meeting my Mr. Right that hasn't worked out? Did I think it would happen before I started grad school? Or was I expecting to at least know my guy before some of my friends got engaged?

I remember a talk I had with my mom after breaking up with Jay. She said that when having something becomes an obsessive desire in the heart of a believer, it represents an idol that's being wor- shipped. I don't want that to happen again. If Jesus came back for His Church at this very moment, I'd instantly leave earth, never knowing what it was like to have a husband and, more importantly, not even caring. You'll be more than enough for me in heaven, and You're more than enough for me now.

You know, Father, I'm gradually learning that only You can truly satisfy. Believing that I need a boyfriend to make me happy or a husband to complete me is wrong. That's too much to expect of anyone except You. Those unrealistic expectations will set me up for disappointment once I am married.

The truth is I'm complete in You, whether or not I have a man in my life. You alone can meet my deepest needs and make me truly happy. I'm comforted to know that You will take care of me no matter what and that You'll never fail me. Forgive me, Lord, if I've looked anywhere but to You for my self worth or for what I really need in life. Once again, I'm reminded why I've chosen to make You my first love.

So from this time on, I purpose in my heart to be content in whatever state I'm in. In my case, that means being single for now. Feeling frustrated because my guy is nowhere in sight may be normal, but it's a waste of time and an insult to You. It also makes it hard for me to be happy for others when they're getting what I want and still don't have.

I mustn't look around anymore and compare my situation with what You're doing in the lives of other Christians. If I do, the Bible says that I'll become a fool. There are plenty of people out there that I can minister to as a single. Help me to take advantage of the opportunities that are before me today. I choose to die to my own desire for immediate gratification, so You can live out Your will through me.

You know my heart, Lord. I still want to become a godly wife and experience all the things You've promised me. And since You've taken care of me in every other way, I'm confident You're taking care of my love life as well. I have nothing to fear, no reason to complain. As long as I'm cooperating with You, I will receive my heart's desire. You're the God of the promise, and I choose to let You be Lord of the timing, too.

I've never thought about this before, but I'm sure life won't be perfect after I've finally met and married my man. There will still be other battles to face and some tears to shed, husband and all. Teach me what I need to learn now, so I can face those challenges as a woman of great faith, a woman who totally trusts in You.

Thanks for helping me straighten out my internal affairs, Father. I love You, and I pray all in Jesus' name.

It was late afternoon when I finished that entry. After I put my journal away, the Holy Spirit reminded me that one of the residents from the Center was still in the hospital recovering from her surgery. I was scheduled to work on Marie's rehab once she was discharged, so I decided to drive over and visit her. On the way, I stopped to pick up some flowers.

I chose a small arrangement of daisies because they had always been my favorite flower. I was definitely looking forward to the time when a handsome man would be bringing *me* daisies. Although I was leaving that floral shop on a mission of mercy, much more was awaiting me at Weston Memorial Hospital.

Déja Vu

The intercom was paging a Dr. Stanton to report to the emergency room when I entered the hospital lobby. "May I help you?" the woman behind the counter asked as I approached the front desk.

"Yes, may I please have the room number for Marie Jensen?"

"Certainly," she answered as she typed in the name and consulted her computer screen. "Room 332. Take the first set of elevators just down that hall," she instructed, pointing the way.

I was already familiar with the layout of the hospital, but I politely thanked the receptionist anyway and started in that direction, repositioning the card and vase of flowers I was carrying so I could operate the elevator. When it stopped on the third floor, I stepped out and walked down a long hallway until I found the right room. Marie's eyes were closed when

I opened the door, so I tiptoed over to the nightstand beside the elderly woman's bed and gently set down the vase.

"Hello, dear. Thank you for the flowers."

Marie's voice startled me, and I jumped, dropping my card on the floor. "Oh, you're welcome," I replied as I stooped down to retrieve the envelope from under a nearby end table. "Sorry if I woke you," I apologized, standing back up and laying the card next to the vase.

"I wasn't really asleep. It's hard to rest for long with this big cast on my leg. My son just left a few minutes ago. I'm afraid he's still a bit annoyed with me because I fell trying to help Hilda get to the toilet. Sometimes I forget I'm an old lady. I still think I can do everything I used to. Only my body can't keep up with my mind anymore. Don't get old, honey. It's not much fun," Marie sighed, struggling to adjust the pillow behind her head.

"Here, let me help you," I quickly offered.

For the next few minutes, I attempted to update Marie on the latest news at the Center, but she had already received a complete report from Miss Lottie earlier that day. Fortunately, I had brought a book of short stories with me, and we spent the next hour reading and laughing together. When I saw Marie was getting tired, I kissed her on the cheek and left to go home.

Reaching the ground floor, I remembered my parents were out for the evening and I was on my own for dinner. Not wanting to make another stop,

I decided to grab something from the hospital cafeteria. I'd eaten there lots of times, and the food was inexpensive. It was a good thing, too. I didn't have that much cash on me after paying for Marie's flowers and card.

Scanning my choices in the cafeteria, I finally decided on a cup of soup and a Caesar salad. "Want a beverage with that?" the cashier asked as I set my tray down.

"Just some ice water, please."

"Over there," she replied, motioning to a drink station in the dining area. "Here's a cup, and you'll find lemon slices on the counter."

"Thanks," I said, digging in my purse for my money. Carrying my tray to the drink station, I got some water and found a table to sit at in the corner of the room. After giving thanks for my food, I pulled out my book and read between bites. Before long, I was completely engrossed in one of the short stories, oblivious to my surroundings.

"Mind if I sit here?" a voice suddenly asked, breaking my concentration. Looking up, I scanned the room to see that the dining area was virtually empty. There were plenty of other seats available. Feeling a bit awkward, I simply nodded my approval as I studied this good-looking young man in the white hospital coat.

Setting his coffee down on the table, he reached over and shook my hand. "I'm David Stanton." Before I could respond, he said, "And you're Julia Duncan, right?"

Taken by surprise, I felt my face flush as I nodded again. Sitting down across from me, he added, "And you're wondering how I know your name, aren't you?"

"Yes," I shyly admitted.

"Well, I know more than your name. I know you're doing your graduate work in P.T., you play racquetball, you're a youth leader at your church...Shall I go on?" he asked, smiling. My expression must have shown that I wasn't amused.

"Hey, I'm sorry, Julia. I'm only teasing, but I think I'm scaring you with all this personal information. Let me explain how I know so much about you. I'm new to Weston, and I just started seeing patients at the Center. Now can you guess where I learned all about you?"

Relieved, I broke out into a knowing grin. "Oh, you've met Miss Lottie."

The doctor laughed. "That's right. She's quite the welcoming committee. She told me about the condos where I'm living now and recommended Weston Christian Center when I asked about a good church."

"Really? I'm surprised. Miss Lottie doesn't even go to our church."

"She told me she would if she were 'a young doctor looking for a pretty woman to keep company with.' She warned me that there were only old ladies at her church."

Now I was laughing. "Isn't she the best? I love that woman. I never thought I would have such a close friend her age."

"Well, she definitely loves you."

"Thanks. How did she end up talking about me, anyway?"

"I was passing by the P.T. unit a couple days ago and saw you working with one of my patients. I stopped at the doorway to watch you for a few seconds. There was something about the way you talked to him that caught my attention. I would've come in and introduced myself, but I was just leaving for the hospital and had to go. The next day I mentioned you to Lottie, and she told me all about you." I just smiled, knowing I'd hear all about *him* as soon as Miss Lottie found out we'd met.

"You're really good with older people," he continued. "When I was in to see the Johnsons yesterday, you walked past their room, and they said you'd led both of them to the Lord."

"Yes, they're such a nice couple. I used to work in their wing my first couple of years at the Center. I still try to come see everyone now and then, but with my schedule in the P.T. unit, I don't have a lot of time for visiting."

"Well, I'm glad I got the chance to meet you, Julia. I'll probably see you at church tomorrow."

"It was nice to meet you, too, Dr. Stanton. I'll look for you and introduce you around after service, if you want."

"Thanks. And do me a favor. Call me by my first name when I'm not at the Center. When I'm not on duty, I'm just David."

"Are you on duty now?"

"No, I'm on my way home. I would've been out of here after making my rounds, but I was paged to the emergency room."

"Nothing serious, I hope."

"No, a little boy wanted to pet his hamster and sliced his finger on the cage instead. Just a few stitches, that's all."

"That's good. Well, I guess I'll say goodnight, David. I'm heading home, too."

"Great—let's walk out together," he suggested, adding his coffee cup to my tray. He carried it over to the conveyer drop-off and then joined me again. As we walked out of the cafeteria, he mentioned that he was a racquetball player, too. "We'll have to play sometime. I haven't been on a court in a few months, so I'm a little out of shape. You'll have to take it easy on me at first."

"Can't make any promises," I laughed, secretly thinking he in no way looked out of shape. He proved me right a few seconds later when he removed his white coat and draped it over his arm. The blue knit shirt he was wearing underneath clung to his torso, suggesting a very nice physique.

We stopped by the doctor's lounge on our way out so David could toss his hospital coat in the laundry bin and pick up his suede jacket. He slipped it on just in time to safely guide me ahead of him through the revolving door as we exited the lobby.

The night air was cool and a little breezy, so I quickly fastened the top button of my coat as we walked. Reaching the parking area, we said good night again and separated to find our cars.

"Remember to look for me in church tomorrow," he reminded me over his shoulder.

As I walked, I couldn't help but smile. David was handsome, charming, *and* a Christian. I wouldn't forget to look for him in the morning. In fact, there would probably be quite a few women noticing him at that church service.

Nearing my vehicle, my smile faded as I spotted a black sedan parked two spaces away. Seeing the Weston U faculty-parking sticker on the windshield, I quickly unlocked my car and opened the door. Feeling the presence of someone directly behind me, I spun around to find Don McNulty standing less than a foot away.

He had me trapped. My door was pushing against the car parked right next to me, and I was wedged inside with no place to run. Panicked, I reached to blow the horn, but McNulty caught my left hand and yanked it away from the steering wheel. He reeked of alcohol.

"What's wrong, Julia?" he said tauntingly, still firmly gripping my wrist. "We haven't had a good talk for a long time, and I miss you. I saw your car here, and I've been waiting for you to come out. We've got some unfinished business between us, don't we?"

"I...I don't know what you mean," I answered, terrified.

"You girls are all the same," he accused. "Turn a man on and then dump him just as fast." Stepping in even closer, he pressed me against the door so I couldn't move.

"Let me go!" I shouted over and over again, trying to pull my arm free.

"Relax, Julia. All I want is a little kiss."

"No! Leave me alone! Let me go!" I screamed, trying to push away from him with all my might, frantically turning my face from side to side to keep him from kissing me. Reaching up, he clutched a fistful of my hair, yanking me towards him. But just before his lips touched mine, he suddenly let me go.

It was then that I saw David. His car was still running with the door flung wide open behind him. He was the one who had pulled McNulty off me, grabbing him and twisting the collar of his coat, cutting off his air.

Dragging the professor to the back of my car, David whipped him around and threw him against the trunk, pinning his shoulders back. "Something wrong with your hearing?" he angrily shouted. "I heard the lady telling you to back off from two aisles away." Shoving the professor away from the car, David ordered him to get lost.

McNulty didn't argue. He just gave us both a dirty look and muttered a few expletives under his breath. He was in his sedan in a matter of seconds, and we watched him as he peeled out of the parking lot.

When the car was out of sight, David turned to find me shaken, barely able to stand. Bracing myself on the door of the car, I said, "Thanks, David. I don't know what he would've done if you hadn't stopped him."

"Come on, you need to sit down," he replied, easing me behind the steering wheel. Leaning down, he asked, "Who was that idiot, anyway? Do you know him?"

"Unfortunately, I do. He's a professor at Weston U. This isn't the first time he's tried to hit on me."

"It better be the last! That guy's dangerous, Julia. And tonight wasn't just a hit; it was an attack." Straightening up, David pulled out his cell phone and dialed 911.

"Are you calling the police?"

"Yeah," he answered, waiting for the operator to pick up.

"Do you think they'll arrest him?"

David didn't have a chance to answer me; the operator was on the line. Walking back and forth outside the car, he explained the reason for his call. When he was done, he came back over to me. "They're sending someone to make out a report. You need what happened tonight on record to prove he's been harassing you."

"You're right," I agreed, still trembling.

David reached down and picked up my purse and keys from the pavement. Joining me in the car, we waited for the police to arrive. Within a few minutes, a squad car pulled up, and David got out to talk with the officer. He explained that I was still pretty shaken, so the officer got into my car to fill out the police report. When he was finished, he told me that if I wanted to press charges, I would have to file a complaint with the Prosecutor's Office.

"That's it?" David asked. "What about arresting the guy?"

"I can't. Not for a misdemeanor like this. As I said, the young lady will have to decide if she wants to pursue him through legal channels. Now, let me get your information as an eye witness." After taking down David's account of what happened, the officer got back into his squad car and left.

David was noticeably annoyed that McNulty was getting off so easy. Turning his attention to me once again, he said, "You're really in no shape to drive. Let's lock up your car, and I'll take you home. All right?"

"Thanks. My dad and I can pick my car up after church tomorrow."

David helped me into the front seat of his car, double-checking that mine was locked before we left. When we pulled into my driveway fifteen minutes later, I saw that the lights were on in the living room. That meant my mom and dad were back from their benefit dinner early.

"Good, my parents are home. Wait until I tell my dad what happened tonight. He'll want to break McNulty's neck."

"That's a good idea, Julia, but he'll have to get in line. Now that I know who he is, I have first dibs on him. Wait here a minute. I'm going to go tell your parents I'm bringing you in. I don't think you should be standing around while we try to explain. You're still pretty weak."

"Okay, you're the doctor."

David got out of the car and walked up to the front stoop. When he rang the bell, my dad answered the door. I lowered the car window to hear David introduce himself and briefly explain what had happened. Then he asked for someone to turn down my bed. I waved to my dad before he disappeared into the house, and David walked back to the car.

"Okay, your dad's getting your room ready," he said as he opened the car door for me. "Do you think you can walk?"

"Sure, I'm fine," I answered, getting out of the car on my own. My confidence proved stronger than my legs, however. After just a few steps, they buckled, and David had to catch me.

"Looks like I'll have to carry you," he concluded, whisking me up in his arms. As we passed through the open front door of the house, I had a quick flashback to the last time a man carried me over a threshold when I was too weak to walk. But I didn't have time to think about that now. My dad had just met us in the foyer.

"Are you all right, Julia?" he asked, very concerned.

"I'm okay, Dad. A little weak, that's all."

Realizing David didn't know where to go next, my dad pointed to the stairs. "Her room's up there. Second door on the right, Dr. uh... Stanton, did you say?"

"Yes, but call me David."

Trying to lighten the mood, he started huffing and puffing about halfway up the long stairway. "Wow!

When I offered to carry you to your room, I had no idea it'd be an Olympic event."

I knew he was teasing, so I played along. "Well, you said you were out of shape, didn't you? This is just a good workout."

He laughed. "Okay, if you say so. But my workouts aren't usually this fun."

My mom was waiting for us at the door to my room. "Just put her there," she said anxiously, motioning to my bed.

David gently lowered me onto the mattress. My mom helped me take off my coat and shoes, and I got under the comforter, clothes and all. David reached for a couple of the accent pillows that had fallen to the floor and slid them under my feet to prop them up. "Just relax and try to get warmed up before you get undressed for bed," David advised. "I think you may still be experiencing some mild shock."

My dad had followed in right behind us, and now that I was settled, both of my parents were anxious to know exactly what had happened. They each found a place to sit on my bed, and David pulled the desk chair over. Once he was seated, I filled my parents in on how I had met David in the cafeteria after my visit with Marie. Then I told them how McNulty took me by surprise in the parking lot and what he'd tried to do.

"My car was parked a few rows over," David inserted. "I was just getting in when I heard Julia scream. By the time I drove over to where she was, that man had already done a good job of terrorizing her. He was about to force a kiss on her when I pulled him off her."

"We don't know how to thank you, David," my dad said gratefully.

"No need to thank me. Actually, I feel kind of bad. I should've walked Julia to her car. But the parking area is so well lit at the hospital, and it wasn't that late, only eight o'clock. I don't know what that guy was thinking, trying something like that where people are coming and going all the time."

"He'd been drinking, David. I could smell it on his breath."

"You're right. I smelled alcohol, too."

My dad stood and started pacing the room, angry but under control. "McNulty's a sick man," he finally pushed out, shaking his head. "We definitely can't have him teaching at the university anymore."

Turning to me, he added, "I'm so glad David was there to stop him, sweetheart. And I thank God you weren't seriously hurt. I wish it had never happened, but since it did, we're going to use it to get him banned from the campus for good. Until tonight, we didn't have any proof that he's been sexually harassing girls in his classes. Now we do. We have an eyewitness. That's if you're willing to help us, David."

"Just tell me when and where, and I'll be there."

"Let's go downstairs and talk about it over a cup of coffee. Once we're out of here, my wife can help Julia get ready for bed."

"Sure, Mr. Duncan." David got up and put the desk chair back where he found it. Then he came over to my bed and gave my hand a reassuring squeeze. "Good night, Julia. You're looking a lot better already; your color's coming back. All you need now is a good night's sleep. Save a seat for me at church tomorrow, okay?" he requested with a smile, pausing at the door on his way out.

"I will. Thanks again for rescuing me."

"My pleasure. See you in the morning."

After my dad and David left, my mom insisted on helping me get out of my clothes and into some pajamas. Once I was finally tucked in, she kissed me good night and left to join the men downstairs.

Lying in the dark, when all was quiet, I took a moment to pray. "*I had the weirdest thing happen to me tonight, Lord. I don't mean about McNulty. Never mind about that. I mean when I met David. It was like reliving the time Jay and I met at The Coffee Cup. It's been years since that happened, but I remember it like it was yesterday. Almost everything tonight with David was the same. Talk about déjà vu. It's so strange, and I'm not sure what it means. Maybe You'll tell me sometime.*

"*Please help Dad to deal with McNulty. The words* firing squad *keep flashing through my mind. Too severe, Lord? Well, please think it over. It may be the best solution...*"

The trauma of the evening had so drained me, I fell asleep before even finishing my prayer. That afternoon I had chosen to die to self and surrender completely to God's will for me—to patiently wait for my guy as long as necessary. Ironically, as I lay there sleeping, I was unaware that one of the most memorable events of my life had just occurred. Although it would take me some time to realize it, I had finally met my Mr. Right.

Yes, my faith and patience had eventually paid off. While I was comfortably resting in my bed, still trusting God to bring me together with my future husband, he was, in fact, downstairs drinking coffee in the house where I'd known my parents' love all my life. Soon I would be experiencing another kind of love—the kind a woman longs for—a love only the right man can give. For me, David would prove to be that man.

To be continued...

Marrying Mr. Right

"Wait!" you may be saying. "Don't stop now; I want to know what happens next!" Then you will want to continue the journey through Julia's life in the final book of the **MR. RIGHT SERIES**, *Marrying Mr. Right*.

Find out how Julia and David eventually get together. Will the path to true love be smooth or a bit rocky? How did David suddenly show up on the scene, anyway? What series of events brought him to Weston Memorial Hospital? And what about Paul? Is he going to simply give in and go back to the West Coast, or will he stay and fight for the girl he loves? Then there's Professor McNulty. What happens to him?

Join in on all the fun and frustration as Julia and David fall in love and finally get married. Meet David's parents and see how Julia fits in with the Stantons. Learn about the call God has on David's life and how it's going to affect Julia after they're married. See if she can actually make it to the altar without enlisting the help of Daryl and Damon again.

If you have just finished *Meeting Mr. Right* without reading the first book in the **MR. RIGHT SERIES**, *Waiting for Mr. Right*, you probably have a few questions, such as: Who's this Jay that Julia keeps talking about? How *did* they meet? What did he do to her that was so terrible? Follow Julia's adventures as she goes away to college for the first time. Meet all her friends and share their lives on campus. You'll come away from her story wiser and with a much better perspective on dating.

Epilogue

As you read this book, did you think about your own spiritual life? Did you already know that God loves you and wants to be close to you—or did the relationship that Julia and her friends had with God seem strange or unattainable? Maybe no one has told you before how much you mean to God.

The Bible says in John 3:16-18: *God loved the world so very, very much that he gave his only Son. Because he did that, everyone who believes in him will not lose his life, but will live forever. God did not send his Son into the world to judge the world. He sent him to save the world. Everyone who believes in the Son will not be judged. But everyone who does not believe in him is judged already, because he does not believe in the name of God's son.* (Worldwide English Version)

These verses tell us that God wants *everyone* to be in His family. Yet not everyone will be. We are all born with a sinful nature that separates us from a holy God—and a sin debt that is too great for anyone to pay. That's why Jesus paid that debt for us on the cross. He paid what we could not. And now we have access to God the Father once again. All that remains is our choice to accept or reject His offer of salvation.

So, if you have never accepted Jesus as your Savior and Lord, you have a decision to make. Ask yourself: *Do I want to run my own life, miss heaven, and experience less than God's best for me right now? Or do I want to receive what Christ did for me and allow God to direct my life from this day forward, letting Him heal my past hurts and design a better future for me?* This choice is yours to make.

If you've already given your life to Jesus and received Him as *Savior*, you have His promise of eternal life in heaven. But it is important to make Christ the *Lord* of your life as well. When Jesus is your Lord, you seek God's will for your life, taking the time to pray, read the Bible, and then *do* what He tells you (to the best of your ability). As you honor God in this way, you will remain under the protective umbrella of His truth and provision. And you will experience the abundant blessings that come through simple faith, trust, and obedience. If you resist this part, however, you will miss out on much of God's best for your life.

How to Receive Jesus as Savior and Lord

If you have never given your life to the Lord but would like to, He is ready and willing to receive you. If you will pray this prayer from your heart, He will give you a new heart that wants to love and serve Him.

Heavenly Father, I come to you in Jesus' name and ask You to forgive me for the things I have done wrong and for wanting to live life my own way. Right now I invite Jesus to come into my heart and take control of my life. I believe that He died on the cross to pay for my sins: past, present and future. I believe that He was raised from the dead and will welcome me in heaven when my earthly life is over. Please help me to live for You and for others. I believe You have heard my prayer and that I have been born of Your Spirit. I confess Jesus as my Lord and Savior, and I am now a Christian, one who follows Christ.

If you have prayed this prayer for the first time or are rededicating your life to the Lord, you need to find a church that teaches the Bible and will help you grow in your relationship with God. You won't be able to reach your full potential without the help of other Christians.

The best way to know God for yourself is to set aside time to study your Bible and pray. Journaling is another way to connect with God as you record your thoughts and prayers. Over time you can see how you've grown and how God continues to take care of you.

From the Authors...

Your Heavenly Father wants you to highly value yourself as He does and learn to say *no* to anything that or anyone who would compromise your purity or put you in harm's way. Thus, the **MR. RIGHT SERIES** was written to reach out to young women everywhere and acknowledge the issues they are facing, to draw them into more intimate fellowship with Him so He can train, protect, and provide for them.

This three-book series is filled with interesting stories that help the reader to visualize and understand moral and spiritual lessons. Although the characters in *Meeting Mr. Right* are fictitious, the events described are true to life and happen every day. As you read the stories in this novel, we hope you were able to feel what these characters felt as they lived through their experiences—that you have learned how important it is to make wise decisions.

The main character of the **MR. RIGHT SERIES** is Julia. Her name means *youthful*. Yet regardless of age, every woman can benefit from these stories as she relates to Julia's dreams, desires, and struggles. Some girls may be looking ahead to what Julia is experiencing, other women are already at that same stage of life, and still others can look back, remember, and encourage younger women who are feeling anxious and forgotten.

   As you observed Julia's relationship with God in this book, how did you relate to her? Are you a Christian, too? If so, what is your level of commitment to God? Is Jesus your Lord as well as your Savior? Would you like to know Him more intimately, seek His presence, and draw on His power to protect and guide you through life the way Julia did? How much of God do *you* want to experience? Our prayer is that you will choose to make Him the Lord of your life and allow Him to design a blessed future for you.

Don't miss any part of Julia's continuing story! The other two novels in the Mr. Right Series are available now.

Who do you know that would love to read this book?

Captivating! I began reading this morning at 7 a.m. and could not put the book down! My mind was reeling with the names of all the people I must tell about this book.

Barbara Rush-Businesswoman

The *Mr. Right* Novel Series

ISBN: 978-1-60683-493-0
Trade Paper, 176 pages

Novel #1
Waiting for Mr. Right

Written by Lisa Raftery and Barbara Precourt

In the first installment of the series, you will meet Julia as she enters her first year of college. It's an exciting time, but she quickly learns that life away from her traditional Christian home is different. In fact, she finds herself compromising her values to try and fit in. One lie leads to another, putting her very life in danger. Although Julia dreams of the day she will walk down the aisle with her Mr. Right, she's got to survive dating first!

ISBN: 978-1-60683-495-4
Trade Paper, 304 pages

Novel #3
Marrying Mr. Right

Written by Lisa Raftery and Barbara Precourt

In this final novel, Julia has met her Mr. Right, but she's still a long way from the altar! You will applaud Julia's courage as she continues to trust God, even when it looks like everything she's hoped for is slipping away. Her faith in God helps her overcome incredible odds and fulfill her lifelong dream of marrying her Mr. Right. Through it all, we learn that anyone can catch your eye, but it takes someone special to capture your heart.

Available now at www.HarrisonHouse.com
and other bookstores nationwide